Oakland - Book One: The East

Oakland
Book 1

Chrome Nyson

Oakland – Book One: The East

© 2026 **Chrome Nyson**

First Edition

ISBN: 979-8-9946456-3-5 (Paperback)

ISBN: 979-8-9946456-4-2 (Hardback)

Published by

Orline Media

United States of America

For Oakland—
past, present, and the stories still breathing.

In East Oakland, the streets don't whisper — they testify.
Survival is the first language. Loyalty is the second.
And every block remembers your name.

— Chrome Nyson

Author's Note

Oakland is more than a place.

It's a pressure cooker. A proving ground. A mirror.

The stories in this book are fictional, but the emotions, the choices, the consequences — they're real. They come from sidewalks that raised people too early, from blocks where loyalty and survival often spoke louder than hope, and from a city that taught resilience the hard way. This trilogy isn't about glorifying struggle. It's about understanding it.

Oakland – Book One: The East begins where foundations are laid— where identity is shaped, where the environment leaves its fingerprints. Each book moves in a different direction, but all roads trace back to the same truth: where you're from never really lets you go.

This is a story about place. About people.

About what it takes to stand when everything around you says fold.

— **Chrome Nyson**

Chapter One

The sun had dropped behind the Oakland hills, leaving Foothill Boulevard dipped in gold and grit. Streetlights buzzed awake one by one, flickering like they had to think twice before committing to their job.

Maya Brooks stepped off the AC Transit bus and inhaled the sharp, familiar cocktail of East Oakland — exhaust, corner-store grease, fresh rain on old pavement, weed from someone's open window.

Home.

Kids blasted Hyphy music from a beat-up Chrysler. A couple oldheads argued outside Kwik Stop about whose mixtape from the '90s never got the shine it deserved. Sirens hummed far off, always part of the soundtrack.

But tonight, the air felt different.

Tight.

Like the city was holding a secret behind its teeth.

Maya felt it. Everybody felt it.

Two cops had been killed last week. The news spun it like a gang ambush, but the streets didn't buy that story. Folks whispered other things — quiet, tight-lipped, paranoid.

Maya crossed onto her block, hoodie up, backpack bouncing against her hip. She had her spoken-word notebook in her hand, flipping through half-finished lines:

Ghost justice roaming in blue… shadows wearing badges too…

She didn't even know what she meant by it yet. She just knew it felt true.

"You hear about Foothill?" a voice asked.

She turned. Malik leaned on the gate, eyes lit by streetlight and worry.

"Hear what?" she asked.

"They say some cops takin' shit into their own hands. Off-the-books type moves. Folks goin' missin'. They ain't just mad about them two dead officers — they out for blood."

Maya's stomach knotted.

Malik lowered his voice.

"And Dre hit me. Said he overheard somethin' at the station. Said it's big. Real big."

Dre. The janitor nobody noticed. The man who swept floors like he was sweeping memories away.

"What'd he hear?" Maya asked.

Malik looked up and down the street before answering.

"Some cops plannin' a hit. On prisoners."

He paused.

"And their families."

Maya's breath froze in her chest.

"That ain't police work," she whispered.

"Nah," Malik said.

"That's vengeance."

A car rolled by slow, tinted windows, music low. Both of them went silent until it disappeared down the block.

Malik leaned in.

"Dre said they gon' make it look like a breakout. Stage the whole thing. Then kill everybody. Like they doin' the city a favor."

Maya felt the world tilt.

"That's murder."

"That's East Oakland at war," Malik corrected.

Maya clutched her notebook tighter.

Some stories write you.

This one was already carving itself into her bones.

And somewhere deep in the city, gears were turning — dirty gears, hidden gears, grinding toward blood.

The shadows on Foothill were no longer just shadows.

They were men with badges.

And they were coming.

Chapter Two

Morning crept into East Oakland slow, like it wasn't sure it wanted to show up. A thin layer of fog clung to the rooftops along International Boulevard, mixing with diesel fumes and the smell of chorizo from the taco truck already open on 38th.

Maya walked with her notebook tucked under her arm, headphones around her neck but no music playing. She liked hearing the city awake. The soft hiss of the street sweeper rolling past. Vendors setting up fruit crates. Someone yelling at their cousin across the street like it was a normal greeting.

Everything felt ordinary.

Everything felt wrong at the same time.

Mrs. Li swept the front of her herbal shop with the same rhythm she had for twenty years. Without looking up, she said:

"You feel that?"

Maya paused. "Feel what?"

Mrs. Li tapped the air with her broom.

"This. The heaviness. Streets get loud when truth stay quiet."

Before Maya could answer, two police cruisers rolled by slow —

the kind of slow that wasn't about patrolling, but watching. Studying. Choosing.

Mrs. Li muttered something in Cantonese that didn't sound flattering.

"When police drive like that," she said softly, "danger already here."

Maya kept walking, a nervous flutter in her stomach.

She found Malik waiting outside the Eastside Collective rec center, perched on the low concrete wall, hoodie up, tapping his foot like he was trying to shake off a thought that wouldn't leave him alone.

"You good?" Maya asked.

"Nope." Malik hopped down. "And I got reason."

He scanned the street before leaning in.

"Dre texted again. Said the cops ain't just plannin'. They settin' dates. Times. Routes."

Maya swallowed. "For the… hit?"

Malik nodded grimly.

"They gon' make it look like somebody tried to break prisoners out. Then kill the inmates. Kill whoever show up to help. Kill whoever convenient."

"Silencing people," Maya whispered.

"Killing people," Malik said. "There's a difference."

Before she could respond, an engine growled around the corner.

A bright-orange Dodge Charger.

The block shifted — people quieted, eyes slid sideways, conversations paused mid-sentence.

Three men stepped out in black hoodies.

Foothill Hyenas.

At the front of them was Silk.

He moved like someone who had already counted every angle of the street, every witness, every escape route. Calm. Too calm.

He greeted Malik with a tilt of his head.

"Morning," Silk said. "Neighborhood look awake, but everybody seem scared."

"Because they are," Malik replied. His tone wasn't disrespectful — just honest.

Silk's eyes flicked toward Maya.

"You the poet, right?"

Maya felt her pulse tick up. "Yeah."

"Your words got around," he said. "You got eyes. And ears."

Silk stepped closer, lowering his voice.

"People go missin' when cops get emotional," he said. "When they stop bein' officers and start bein' executioners."

Maya felt her throat tighten.

"How much you know?" Malik asked.

Silk shrugged. "Enough to stay out the way. Enough to tell y'all do the same."

"We *are* staying out the way," Malik said.

Silk chuckled — not mocking, just knowing.

"No," he said. "You two stay right at the damn center without even tryin'."

The silence after that felt heavy.

Silk stepped back toward his Charger.

"One more thing," he said. "If you hear about movement on Foothill Friday morning… don't be anywhere near it."

The Hyenas loaded back into the Charger.

The engine roared.

The neighborhood resumed its noise — but quieter this time, like voices lowered out of respect for a warning they didn't hear but somehow felt.

Malik rubbed the back of his neck.

"When someone like Silk show up just to tell you 'be careful'… yeah, somethin' big is coming."

Maya looked down at her notebook, at the half-finished line she wrote the night before.

Shadows wearing badges…

Secrets dressed in blue…

For the first time, she wondered if her words were predicting something instead of describing it.

And if so…
What else was about to come true?

Chapter Three

The Invisible ManDre Whittaker moved through the police station with the quiet certainty of someone who had learned how to be invisible.

Not timid.

Invisible.

Like air. Like shadow. Like background noise people stop hearing once it's always there.

Officers joked loudly by the break room. Phones rang. Radios crackled with half-finished codes and bored dispatch voices. Paperwork shuffled with impatient sighs. Fluorescent lights buzzed overhead like they resented being alive.

But no one looked at Dre.

No one ever did.

And that, tonight, mattered more than anything.

He pushed his mop bucket down the hallway, humming under his breath — low, tuneless, just enough to blend into the building's mechanical rhythm.

But his mind wasn't here.

His mind was replaying voices.

Words.

Plans.

Murder disguised as procedure.

He slowed near the evidence room.

The door was cracked just enough for sound to leak out — tense voices, hushed but heated.

Sergeant Tate. Officer Briggs. Officer Donovan. Others.

Dre's pulse tightened.

He adjusted his grip on the mop handle, posture slouched just enough to look unthreatening, unimportant.

"…transfer is Friday morning. 06:15," Tate said, voice cold as sheet metal.

Briggs exhaled sharply. "We hit them on the route. Quick. Clean. Nobody sees our faces. Make it look like someone tried to break the inmates out."

"Then we take care of the prisoners," Donovan added, quieter. "'Loose ends' included."

Loose ends.

Families.

Witnesses.

Dre's jaw flexed.

"They want an excuse," Tate said. "This gives it to them."

"People been asking questions," another officer muttered.

"We shut that down too," Briggs snapped.

Dre forced himself to keep moving.

Never linger.

Never react.

Invisibility required discipline.

He turned the corner, conversation fading behind him — but not leaving him.

Inside his supply closet, he shut the door softly and leaned back against it.

His heart pounded once.

Twice.

Then steadied.

He exhaled slowly — not fear leaving his body, but anger settling into focus.

He crossed the small closet and knelt beside a stack of old cardboard boxes labeled ARCHIVE CLEANING SUPPLIES — 2008.

He pushed them aside.

Behind them was a loose metal panel in the wall — scratched, repainted, but still removable if you knew where to press.

No one else knew.

No one else ever looked long enough to care.

He slid the panel aside.

Darkness opened.

And inside that darkness… history.

Dre reached in and pulled out a duffel bag.

Heavy.

He set it on the floor and unzipped it slowly.

Inside:

Ammo boxes.

Encrypted radios.

Flash suppressors.

Tactical gloves.

Body armor wrapped in old cloth.

Not new equipment.

Maintained equipment.

Prepared equipment.

He ran his hand over the metal.

Cold.

Familiar.

He closed his eyes.

And for a moment…

He wasn't in a janitor's closet anymore.

***

West Oakland — 1996

The warehouse smelled like rust and rain.

Broken windows let in strips of moonlight that cut across the concrete floor like prison bars. Dre stood with his back straight, hands loose at his sides, breathing slow like Lewis taught him.

"Again," Lewis said.

Dre lunged.

Lewis stepped aside effortlessly and swept Dre's legs, dropping him hard onto the mat.

Dre groaned.

Lewis didn't offer a hand up.

"You moving like you angry," Lewis said. "Anger telegraphs."

Dre pushed himself up. "People dying out here. Hard not to be angry."

Lewis nodded.

"But protection ain't revenge," he said. "You fight for control. Not release."

The other trainees moved in silence around them — dock workers, security guards, former soldiers — all men who loved Oakland enough to train for the day the city might stop loving them back.

Dre wiped sweat from his brow.

"Why you teaching us this?" he asked.

Lewis looked toward the open warehouse doors — toward the distant skyline flickering with police lights.

"Because one day," Lewis said quietly, "the violence won't come from the streets."

Dre frowned. "Where it come from then?"

Lewis met his eyes.

"From people wearing permission."

The words stuck.

Years later, Dre would realize that was the night he stopped training to fight criminals…

…and started training to survive systems.

***

Back in the present, Dre opened his eyes inside the janitor closet.

The duffel bag sat open in front of him like a confession he never meant to make again.

He had promised himself he buried this life.

Promised after Lewis died.

Promised after the last operation went wrong and two boys who weren't supposed to be near the warehouse got caught in crossfire meant for nobody.

He zipped the bag halfway.

Paused.

Then opened it again.

Some wars don't ask if you retired.

They show up anyway.

He reached deeper into the wall cavity and pulled out two more duffel bags.

Prepared.

Maintained.

Waiting.

Everything the counter-attackers would need if the city crossed the line Dre prayed it wouldn't.

He sealed the panel shut and wiped sweat from his brow.

Then he reached into his pocket and pulled out a cheap flip phone — untraceable, disposable.

He typed one message:

FRIDAY. 06:15. EAST ROUTE.

THEY MOVING IN BLOOD.

BE READY.

He hit send.

Outside, a patrol cruiser rolled into the lot, headlights sweeping the walls.

Officers laughed down the hallway.

A printer jammed loudly.

Life went on.

But Dre felt the shift.

Just like Maya.

Just like Malik.

Something dark beneath Oakland had started to unstitch itself.

He grabbed his mop, reopened the closet door, and stepped back into invisibility.

A storm was coming.

And Dre Whittaker wasn't about to let it wash the wrong people away.

Chapter Four

The old oak tree stood in the center of Fremont Park like it had been there long before Oakland had streets, bus lines, or stories to tell.

Its trunk was thick and weathered, bark carved with decades of names, dates, memorials, and confessions. Initials wrapped in hearts. Candle wax melted into the grooves. Faded photographs stapled low near the roots — faces of people gone too soon.

The tree didn't just stand in the park.

It held it together.

Its roots pushed up through the soil like veins, cracking the pavement in slow defiance, reminding everyone that something older than concrete lived beneath the city.

Maya sat beneath its branches, notebook open on her lap, pen resting against the page without moving.

The wind shook loose brittle leaves that spiraled down around her like tired memories.

She came here whenever her mind got crowded.

Whenever the city felt too loud.

Whenever grief, anger, or confusion needed somewhere quiet to land.

The oak had a way of absorbing all of it without asking questions.

She leaned back against the bark and exhaled slowly.

From here, she could see the whole park.

Kids chasing each other near the swing set.

An elder feeding pigeons near the fountain.

Two teens arguing over a speaker playing old Too $hort low enough not to draw police attention.

Normal life.

But even that felt thinner lately — like joy walking on eggshells.

Maya flipped to a fresh page and wrote:

Roots remember what streets forget.

She stared at the line.

Then added:

And the soil don't lie.

Footsteps crunched softly behind her.

"You beat me here."

Malik dropped onto the grass beside her, stretching his legs out like he'd been walking for hours.

She closed her notebook halfway. "Couldn't stay in the house. Feels like the whole city humming."

"Yeah," Malik said quietly. "Like when power lines buzz before a storm."

He picked at the grass absently.

"Dre texted again."

Maya's pulse picked up.

"What now?"

Before Malik could answer, another set of footsteps approached — slower, heavier, measured.

Dre.

Hands tucked deep in his jacket pockets, shoulders carrying weight he hadn't fully decided to share yet.

He didn't sit.

He stood in front of them like someone delivering news that couldn't be softened.

"It's confirmed," Dre said.

Malik straightened. "What is?"

"Friday morning. 06:15. Transfer van. East route. They staging everything."

Maya felt her throat tighten.

"Staging… how?"

"Smoke grenades. Masked shooters. Roadblock chaos," Dre said. "Make it look like a jailbreak attempt. News gon' run it before facts even wake up."

"And then?" Malik asked, though he already knew.

Dre looked between them.

"Then they kill the prisoners. Then whoever connected to 'em. Families if they feel like it."

Maya's stomach dropped.

"And nobody questions it," she whispered.

"Not if they sell the story right," Dre said. "Fear make people accept anything."

The wind moved through the oak branches above them, leaves rattling like whispers arguing.

A voice came from behind:

"For folks planning to save the city, y'all real loud."

They turned.

Silk stood near the edge of the grass, hands in his hoodie pockets, head tilted slightly like he'd been listening for longer than he let on.

Malik tensed immediately.

"You follow us?"

Silk shrugged. "Didn't need to. Word travel fast on Foothill. Plus y'all picked the most obvious meeting tree in the East."

He stepped closer, gaze lifting briefly to the branches above.

"My mama used to bring me here," he said quietly. "Said this tree older than city politics. Older than police budgets. Older than lies."

Maya studied him.

It was the first time she'd heard softness in his voice.

"You believe that?" she asked.

Silk smirked faintly. "I believe trees see everything. Just don't testify."

Dre didn't smile.

"Why you here?"

Silk looked back at him.

"Same reason as you," he said. "City shifting. Lines moving. And people like Tate? They don't move unless somebody higher give 'em permission."

Maya frowned. "Higher like who?"

Silk glanced toward the skyline beyond the park.

"You ever notice how whole blocks get cleared right before developers announce projects?" he asked.

Malik nodded slowly.

"Yeah…"

Silk pointed subtly toward the streets surrounding the park.

"Three blocks east already rezoned. Two more approved. Tech investors buying property quiet."

Maya felt it click.

"You saying this hit… tied to gentrification?"

Silk didn't answer directly.

He just said:

"Fear lower property value. Violence justify displacement. Police get overtime. Developers get land."

Dre exhaled slowly.

"I figured as much."

Silk looked back at Maya.

"You writing all this down?"

"Not yet," she said.

"You should," he replied. "Truth disappear fast when money involved."

Malik stood.

"So what — you offering to help now?"

Silk smirked slightly.

"I didn't say that. I just said y'all gon' need it."

He stepped closer to Maya, voice lower now.

"And if things go bad Friday — and they will — you keep that notebook close. Words outlive bullets."

The statement sat heavy between them.

He stepped back.

"Be safe," Silk said. "Or be gone. Ain't no middle ground this week."

He turned and walked off the way he came — silent, deliberate, like the streets bent around his presence.

Malik watched him go.

"We really taking advice from him now?"

"We not taking advice," Dre said. "We taking information."

Maya leaned back against the oak again, looking up into the branches.

For a moment…

The sounds of the park faded.

And memory slipped in.

***

She was eight years old.

Sitting beneath this same tree with her grandmother.

Back when the bark felt smoother.

Back when the carvings weren't so many.

Her grandmother handed her a notebook — cheap spiral-bound, purple cover.

"Write what you see," she said.

Maya frowned. "Why?"

"Because stories keep people alive longer than bodies do," her grandmother replied.

A siren wailed somewhere in the distance.

Young Maya flinched.

Her grandmother didn't.

"City always gon' have noise," she said. "Your job is to hear what's underneath it."

Maya looked up at the branches.

"What this tree hear?"

Her grandmother smiled.

"Everything."

***

Back in the present, Maya blinked slowly.

The wind rustled again — stronger this time.

Leaves spiraled down around the three of them like warnings.

She looked at Malik.

Then Dre.

Then the city skyline beyond the park.

"I think this tree been watching this story longer than we have," she said quietly.

Dre nodded once.

"Then we better make sure it don't end wrong."

Maya closed her notebook, stood, and slid the pen behind her ear.

Fear was still there.

Heavy.

But something else had taken root beside it.

Purpose.

Whatever was coming Friday…

Whatever storm was building beneath police radios and city hall meetings…

She knew one thing now.

They weren't just reacting anymore.

They were stepping into it.

She looked back once at the oak tree before leaving the park.

Its branches swayed slowly overhead, casting shadows that stretched long across the grass like arms trying to hold the neighborhood together.

Maya whispered to herself:

"Then we prepare."

Chapter Five

The old rec center on 47th had been abandoned long enough for the neighborhood to forget its real purpose.

Once, kids ran full-court games inside its walls. Elders voted here during elections. Summer programs filled the rooms with laughter, arguments, and sneaker squeaks echoing off polished wood floors.

Now the windows were boarded.

Murals on the exterior had faded into sun-bleached ghosts — community heroes, Black Panthers, local legends barely visible beneath peeling paint.

Time hadn't erased the building.

It had hollowed it out.

Tonight, one thin strip of light leaked from a broken window, slicing through the darkness like the building itself was waking back up.

Inside, dust floated in the air like ash after a fire.

The floorboards creaked under every step.

The silence felt intentional — like the building knew it wasn't supposed to be alive again.

Maya stood just inside the doorway, arms folded against the cold.

Her notebook sat in her back pocket, but her fingers kept brushing it unconsciously, grounding herself.

This place felt different than the park.

Heavier.

Like decisions made here couldn't be undone.

Malik paced the open gym floor, restless energy pouring off him.

"Man… this really where we doin' this?"

His voice echoed through the rafters.

Amina sat at a folding table she dragged from a storage closet, laptop open, cords sprawled like vines across the dusty floor.

Her fingers moved fast, eyes flicking between screens.

"I boosted signal using an old relay tower near MacArthur," she said without looking up. "If OPD chatter spikes, I'll hear it."

DeShawn leaned against the far wall cracking his knuckles rhythmically.

Rico stood near the entrance shadows, silent, watchful — the type who measured rooms before trusting them.

Then the doors creaked open again.

Dre stepped inside carrying two duffel bags.

Heavy ones.

He set them on the center table with a thud that echoed through the gym.

"Gear," he said simply.

Malik stopped pacing.

"What kind of gear?"

Dre unzipped the first bag.

Inside:

Radios.

Flashlights.

Smoke canisters.

Gloves.

Zip ties.

Tactical vests.

Items civilians didn't casually own.

DeShawn let out a low whistle.

"Ain't no way this legal."

"Ain't nothin' about Friday legal," Dre replied.

He opened the second bag.

Weapons.

Not military-grade — but serious enough that nobody mistook their purpose.

Maya flinched instinctively.

Malik stepped slightly in front of her without thinking.

"You good?"

She swallowed.

"I knew it was serious but… seeing it? It's different."

Dre's voice softened.

"These ain't for startin' a war," he said. "They for makin' sure you walk home after one."

Silence settled heavy across the room.

Amina spoke without looking up.

"They changed radio frequencies. Twice. That means they mobilizing units they don't want traced."

DeShawn pushed off the wall.

"So it's real real."

"Yeah," Dre said. "It is."

A long pause followed — the kind where nobody wanted to speak first because speaking made it irreversible.

Then:

Knock. Knock.

Everyone froze.

Rico's hand slid toward his waistband.

Dre held up a hand.

"Relax."

The door creaked open slowly.

Silk stepped inside.

His presence shifted the room instantly — not loud, not aggressive, just undeniable gravity.

"Damn," he said, scanning the gym. "Y'all really set up headquarters in a haunted YMCA."

Malik groaned.

"How you keep finding us?"

Silk smirked.

"I know every abandoned building in the East with a broken lock. Comes with the territory."

He walked to the table, eyes skimming the weapons.

"So this the plan? Y'all meet the cops head-on?"

"This ain't your business," Dre said flatly.

Silk raised an eyebrow.

"My neighborhood, ain't it?" He nodded toward Maya. "Her neighborhood too. Everybody we love live on these streets."

He turned serious.

"And if them cops get away with Friday? None of us safe no more."

Amina looked up finally.

"You offering help or commentary?"

Silk leaned against the table casually.

"Whatever y'all doin', y'all ain't ready."

Malik crossed his arms.

"And you are?"

Silk shrugged.

"More than you."

The tension spiked — but Silk lifted a hand before it boiled.

"Relax. I ain't here to take over. I just don't wanna read about y'all dying in the Chronicle next week."

Rico spoke for the first time.

"What you know we don't?"

Silk's eyes moved to Dre.

"You planning for cops," he said quietly. "But this ain't just cops."

Maya felt her stomach drop.

"Meaning?"

Silk paused — measuring how much truth to drop at once.

"They hired contractors."

The room went still.

"Private military," he continued. "Ex-special forces. Folks who don't wear badges, don't file reports, don't hesitate."

A chill ran through Maya's spine.

Dre's jaw tightened.

"You sure?"

Silk nodded once.

"I got sources. Ridge positions already scoped."

DeShawn muttered under his breath:

"This just went from bad to biblical."

***

Dre stepped forward, voice steady again.

"Aight. Then we stop thinkin' like civilians."

He began distributing gear.

Radios to DeShawn and Rico.

Vest to Malik.

Backup comms to Amina.

Maya watched it all like someone observing the birth of something dangerous.

Silk studied her.

"You scared?"

She nodded honestly.

"Yeah."

"Good," he said. "Fear keep you alive. Just don't let it freeze you."

He turned back to Dre.

"Time short. Training start tonight."

Malik looked around the dusty gym.

"Training? In here?"

Silk grinned.

"Ain't about the building. It's about the people."

He clapped once.

"Aight," Silk said. "Let's get to work."

***

Hours passed.

The rec center stopped feeling abandoned.

It started feeling activated.

DeShawn and Rico practiced entry drills through a rusted side door Dre rigged upright.

Malik learned radio call signs and response codes.

Amina built signal jammers from repurposed parts.

Dre moved between everyone like a coach who never retired — correcting stances, adjusting timing, sharpening instincts.

Maya stayed near the wall, watching.

Learning.

Recording mentally.

Silk eventually stood beside her.

"You ain't gotta fight," he said.

"I know," she replied. "But I still gotta understand."

He pointed across the gym.

"See how Rico move? Always sideways? That's blind-spot movement."

He pointed to Amina.

"She filtering signal from noise. Hardest battlefield skill there is."

Then Malik.

"He got heart. But heart get you killed if discipline don't sit next to it."

Maya looked up at Silk.

"And you? What you got?"

Silk smiled faintly.

"I got history."

Before she could ask more —

Amina stiffened at her laptop.

"Uh… Dre?"

He walked over immediately.

"What happened?"

She adjusted her headphones, replaying intercepted chatter.

Static.

Encrypted bursts.

Then one phrase broke through:

"Friday parameters expanded. Additional units authorized. Execute full purge protocol."

Silence swallowed the gym.

Malik whispered:

"Full what?"

Amina replayed it again.

Dre's face hardened.

Silk muttered under his breath.

DeShawn asked:

"What that mean?"

Dre answered slowly.

"It means they ain't just hitting the prisoners."

Maya felt her pulse spike.

"Who else?"

Dre met her eyes.

"Witnesses. Informants. Affiliates. Anybody connected. Anybody inconvenient."

Malik stepped forward, panic creeping in.

"My grandma live on Foothill."

Rico clenched his jaw.

"My auntie too."

Silk stared at the wall like he wanted to punch through it.

Dre zipped the weapon bag shut.

Then the gear bag.

His voice dropped low — heavy enough to shake the room.

"We got two days," he said.

"Two days to stop something meant to erase half the East."

A siren wailed outside.

Long.

Lonely.

And for the first time…

Nobody heard it as background noise.

They heard it as a countdown.

Friday wasn't an ambush anymore.

It was a massacre in the making.

Chapter Six

The rec center didn't feel abandoned anymore.

Not once the drills started.

Dust still floated in the air, catching in the broken light beams slicing through cracked windows — but the silence that once lived here was gone.

Replaced by movement.

Commands.

Footsteps.

The sound of fear turning into preparation.

Dre stood at the center of the gym floor, arms crossed, watching everyone like a man measuring not skill — but survival instinct.

Years ago, before he became "the janitor," he trained people for situations the news never reported.

Situations that didn't have clean endings.

Tonight, that version of him had come back.

And he didn't look comfortable wearing it again.

"Spread out," Dre said. "Every corner of this building got strengths and weaknesses. Learn both."

Rico and DeShawn ran breach drills using a rusted maintenance door Dre had ripped from its hinges and propped upright with cinderblocks.

"Low entry," Dre barked.

They moved in sync — shoulder first, pivot, clear angles.

"Too slow," Dre snapped.

They reset.

Again.

Harder this time.

Their boots echoed through the hollow gym like distant thunder.

Across the room, Amina sat cross-legged on the floor surrounded by tech gear that looked scavenged from three different decades.

Signal boosters.

Frequency scramblers.

Portable antennas.

Her laptop screen flickered with encrypted chatter she was trying to crack in real time.

She lived in a different battlefield than the others — invisible, digital, but just as lethal.

Malik adjusted the tactical vest Dre handed him earlier.

It hung heavy on his shoulders.

Not physically.

Symbolically.

"You sure this necessary?" he asked quietly.

Dre walked up and tugged the vest tighter.

"You wanna come home Friday?"

Malik swallowed.

"Yeah."

"Then yeah," Dre said.

He stepped back.

"Get used to the weight. Fear heavier than that if you let it sit."

Malik nodded slowly.

Across the gym, Maya leaned against the wall watching everything unfold.

Her notebook sat open in her hands, but she wasn't writing poetry tonight.

She was writing observations.

Movements.

Timing.

Faces under stress.

This was research now.

Documentation.

She didn't belong on the front line — but she was realizing she belonged in the war all the same.

Silk noticed her watching instead of training.

He walked over quietly.

"You ain't gotta do hands-on," he said.

"I know," she replied. "But I gotta understand what y'all walking into."

Silk nodded.

He pointed toward Rico.

"See how he move sideways? That ain't random. That's blind-spot navigation. Harder to target."

He pointed to Amina.

"She fighting with signals instead of fists. Might be the most important role in here."

Then Malik.

"He got heart. Heart get people killed if discipline don't ride shotgun."

Maya looked up at Silk.

"And you?"

Silk's expression shifted slightly.

"I got experience," he said first.

Then added softer:

"And regrets."

Before Maya could ask what he meant —

Dre clapped sharply.

"Switch partners!"

Malik groaned.

"Man why I gotta train with Rico again?"

Rico smirked.

"Because you keep dropping your guard."

"On three," Dre commanded. "Move!"

They collided into grappling drills — controlled but intense.

Rico swept Malik's legs the first round.

Malik hit the floor hard.

"Damn!"

"You hesitate," Rico said, offering a hand up. "You lose."

They reset.

Faster this time.

Stronger.

Maya watched, realizing something unsettling:

They were getting better.

Not playing.

Not pretending.

Preparing.

***

Dre suddenly tossed a metal pipe across the gym floor.

BANG.

The noise cracked like a gunshot.

Everyone reacted.

DeShawn dropped low instantly.

Rico pivoted into cover stance.

Amina flinched but stayed seated.

Malik jumped — just slightly — but recovered fast.

Silk didn't move at all.

Dre nodded.

"Reflex check," he said.

He tossed another pipe.

BANG.

No one flinched this time.

"Better," Dre said.

Silk glanced at Malik.

"You learning."

Malik shot him a look.

"You still ain't answered why you helping us."

Silk paused.

For a long moment.

Then answered honestly:

"Because I know how it feel when the city decide you disposable."

Maya felt that land heavy.

There was more to Silk's story.

A lot more.

But tonight wasn't the night to dig it up.

***

Hours passed.

Sweat replaced dust in the air.

Breathing got heavier.

Muscles tired.

But nobody quit.

Because quitting meant accepting Friday's outcome.

And none of them were ready to do that.

Then —

Amina froze mid-typing.

Her face drained of color.

"Dre…"

He walked over fast.

"What you got?"

She adjusted her headphones, isolating a channel buried under encryption.

Static filled the speakers.

Then voices.

Low.

Coded.

Military cadence.

She boosted the audio.

"…Friday parameters expanded. Additional units authorized. Execute full purge protocol."

Silence swallowed the room.

Malik blinked.

"Full what?"

Amina replayed it.

Same message.

Same tone.

Dre's jaw tightened hard enough to crack teeth.

Silk muttered under his breath.

DeShawn stepped forward.

"What that mean?"

Dre exhaled slowly.

"It means this ain't just a prisoner hit anymore."

Maya felt her pulse spike.

"Then what is it?"

Dre looked around the room before answering.

"It's a city cleanse."

Nobody spoke.

Nobody breathed.

He continued:

"Witnesses. Informants. Families. Affiliates. Anyone connected. Anyone who might talk after."

Malik stepped forward fast.

"My grandma live on Foothill."

Rico clenched his fists.

"My auntie too."

DeShawn muttered:

"They talking genocide with badges."

Silk stared at the wall like he wanted to punch through it.

"They escalating because they scared," he said quietly.

Dre zipped the gear bag shut.

Then the weapons bag.

His voice dropped low — but carried weight.

"We got two days," he said.

"Two days to stop something designed to erase half the East."

Outside, a siren wailed long and hollow.

Nobody ignored it this time.

It sounded less like emergency response…

And more like a countdown.

Maya closed her notebook slowly.

Fear still lived in her chest.
But it had changed shape.
It wasn't paralyzing anymore.
It was directional.
Focused.
She wasn't just documenting history now.
She was inside it.
And Friday…
Friday was coming whether they were ready or not.

Chapter Seven

Thursday evening slid into Oakland like a slow, heavy shadow.

Clouds hung low over the East, thick enough to swallow the moon whole. The sky looked bruised — purple and gray — like even the weather felt what was coming.

Maya felt it the moment she stepped outside.

People moved differently.

Porch lights flicked on earlier than usual. Storefronts closed faster. Conversations happened in low tones, shoulders turned inward like folks were trying to make themselves smaller.

Fear didn't scream in East Oakland.

It whispered.

She pulled her hoodie tighter and walked toward Foothill.

Every passing car made her glance twice.

Every siren made her chest tighten.

This wasn't paranoia.

This was instinct.

She spotted Malik waiting at the corner of 46th and Foothill, leaning against a light pole, dressed head-to-toe in black — nothing flashy, nothing tactical, just street gear meant to blend into darkness.

He looked tired.
Not physically.
Mentally.
"You ready?" he asked when she reached him.
Maya didn't answer right away.
She watched a mother usher her kids inside a corner store faster than usual.
Watched an old man lock his gate twice.
Then she exhaled.
"No."
Malik nodded once.
"Good," he said. "Means you understand what tomorrow is."
They started walking toward the rec center.
Neither spoke for a few blocks.
Words felt unnecessary.
The city was speaking loud enough on its own.
***
Inside the rec center, the atmosphere had shifted from training ground…
…to war room.
Maps covered the folding tables.
Street layouts.
Police patrol routes.
Transit schedules.
Surveillance blind spots.
Dre stood at the center of it all, coffee in hand, though the cup had gone cold hours ago.
Amina worked both laptops simultaneously, signal interceptors humming beside her like mechanical insects.
Rico and DeShawn checked radios and spare batteries.
Silk leaned against the far wall, silent, watching everything like a chess player studying the board before the first move.
No one joked tonight.
No one laughed.
This was the last calm moment they would get.
Dre tapped the map.

"Transfer van leaves city jail 06:15 sharp," he said. "Escort vehicles front and rear. Standard protocol until they hit the choke point here."

He circled a narrow roadway flanked by ridges.

"Once they enter this corridor, Tate's unit stages the fake breakout."

Malik shook his head slowly.

"Calling it 'fake breakout' still sound insane."

"Because it is," Dre replied.

Amina looked up from her screen.

"Encrypted chatter confirms contractor presence on the ridge line," she said. "Private military. No badge IDs."

Rico scoffed.

"So cops hired soldiers to kill prisoners."

Silk spoke without moving from the wall.

"Not hired," he said. "Authorized."

Everyone looked at him.

He continued:

"When contractors show up, it means somebody above Tate signed off."

Maya felt a chill crawl up her spine.

"How high up?" she asked.

Silk didn't answer directly.

"High enough that police reports already written."

The room went quiet.

Dre cleared his throat.

"Which is why tomorrow ain't about outshooting them," he said. "It's about disrupting the choreography."

He pointed to two positions:

"The ridge."

"The roadway."

"Silk handles movement inside the smoke," Dre said.

Silk nodded once.

"I create confusion," he said. "Break their timing."

"Amina jams comms for sixty seconds," Dre continued.

"Sixty seconds is all I can hold before they reroute," she

confirmed.

"Enough," Dre said.

He turned to Rico and DeShawn.

"You two assist prisoner extraction if opportunity presents itself."

Both nodded.

Then Dre looked at Maya.

His tone softened.

"You don't engage," he said. "You document. Cameras, time-stamps, faces, badge numbers if visible. Proof is your weapon."

Maya swallowed but nodded.

She understood now.

Her notebook wasn't protection anymore.

Her footage was.

***

A heavy silence settled over the room.

The plan was real now.

No more theory.

No more rehearsal.

This was happening in less than twelve hours.

Malik rubbed his hands together.

"Anybody else feel like this city holding its breath?"

"Because it is," Silk said quietly.

He stepped away from the wall and walked toward the map.

"Tomorrow don't end anything," he said. "It exposes something."

He tapped the ridge line.

"These contractors? They ain't from Oakland. But somebody invited them."

He tapped the transport route.

"Tate ain't acting solo. He too confident."

He stepped back.

"This is bigger than revenge."

Maya spoke before she could stop herself.

"Then what is it?"

Silk met her eyes.

"Control," he said. "Control through fear. Fear through violence. Violence through narrative."

Dre nodded slowly.

"They make the East look lawless," he said. "Then they justify flooding it."

Amina added quietly:

"And redevelopment follows."

Maya felt sick.

So this wasn't just vengeance.

It was restructuring.

Erasure disguised as safety.

***

One by one, the group began packing gear for morning deployment.

Radios clipped.

Batteries pocketed.

Masks folded.

Maya stepped outside for air.

The night felt colder now.

She leaned against the wall and opened her notebook.

For the first time since this started…

…she didn't write poetry.

She wrote names.

Times.

Locations.

This wasn't art anymore.

This was evidence.

Footsteps approached.

She looked up.

Silk stood beside her.

"You scared?" he asked.

She nodded.

"Yeah."

He didn't smile.

"Good," he said. "Fear mean you understand the stakes."

She studied him.

"You don't seem scared."

Silk exhaled slowly.

"I been scared since 2009," he said. "You just get used to carrying it quieter."

She didn't ask what happened in 2009.

She knew she'd learn soon enough.

He looked toward the skyline.

"If things go bad tomorrow…" he said, "…you run."

"I'm not running," she said.

He glanced at her.

"You got proof, not protection. Know the difference."

She nodded reluctantly.

Inside, Dre called out:

"Wrap it up. Everyone get rest if you can."

No one believed sleep was coming.

Still…

They tried.

Because dawn was already on its way.

And when it arrived…

Oakland wouldn't wake up the same city it went to bed as.

Chapter Eight

F riday dawned gray and undecided.

Fog clung low over East Oakland like the sky hadn't finished forming yet. Streetlights still glowed faint in the early morning haze, casting halos through the mist.

The city felt suspended between night and day.

Between quiet and violence.

Between breath and impact.

At the city jail loading bay, the transport van idled with a low mechanical growl.

Exhaust curled into the cold air.

Two escort vehicles flanked it — lights off, engines running, officers moving with rehearsed calm that masked something darker underneath.

Sergeant Marcus Tate checked his watch.

06:07.

He scanned the lineup with surgical stillness.

"Briggs, you take point," Tate said.

Officer Briggs nodded, adjusting his vest.

"Donovan, rear escort."

Donovan swallowed before answering.

"Yes, sir."

"Marquez, ridge overwatch. Contractors deploy when we reach corridor."

Marquez's voice crackled through comms.

"Copy that."

Tate stepped closer to the van, placing his hand on the cold metal like a priest blessing a coffin.

"Once we start," he said quietly, "there is no hesitation. No mercy. No mistakes."

He looked directly at Donovan.

"You understand?"

Donovan forced the nod.

"Yes, sir."

Inside the van, shackled inmates shifted uneasily.

They couldn't hear the full plan.

But they could feel the tension.

Prisoners always could.

06:14.

Tate gave a single nod.

"Roll."

The convoy pulled out.

Slow.

Controlled.

Deadly in intention.

And Oakland… kept waking up, unaware.

***

Two miles east, Dre lay prone behind a crumbled concrete barrier overlooking the designated choke point.

Binoculars steady.

Breathing slow.

Years of buried training resurfacing without permission.

He watched the convoy snake through the fog below.

"They're rolling," he whispered into his mic.

Amina's voice crackled in his ear.

"Copy. Radio traffic still clean. They haven't flipped channels yet."

Down the slope, Malik crouched behind a rusted guardrail with Rico beside him.

Both dressed dark.

Both masked.

Both vibrating with adrenaline.

"You good?" Rico asked quietly.

Malik exhaled.

"Nope."

Rico smirked.

"Good. Means you ain't stupid."

Across the road, half-hidden beside a broken-down Civic parked at an angle…

Silk leaned casually against the hood.

Hands in pockets.

Posture loose.

Eyes razor sharp.

He watched the convoy approach like a man watching history line itself up for interruption.

They always pick roads nobody cares about, he thought.

Forgotten asphalt.

Forgotten people.

Forgotten accountability.

***

Farther back, Maya and Amina stayed behind a low retaining wall.

Maya held her handheld camera in one hand and her phone in the other — both recording.

Her hands shook.

Her framing didn't.

"You keep filming no matter what," Amina whispered.

Maya nodded.

Even if it gets loud.

Even if it gets ugly.

Even if I don't want to see it.

She zoomed in on the convoy headlights emerging through the fog.

This wasn't theory anymore.
This was happening.
***
High on the ridge, contractors moved into position.
No badges.
No names.
Faces partially obscured.
Rifles steady.
Professional.
Detached.
Officer Marquez adjusted his scope beside them.
He didn't like working with contractors.
But he liked the mission.
Tate's voice crackled through encrypted comms.
"All units report."
"Ridge in place," Marquez replied.
"Escort ready," Briggs said.
"Rear secure," Donovan added, voice tight.
Tate smiled faintly inside his unmarked vehicle trailing behind the formation.
"On my mark," he said.
"We make history."
***
The convoy entered the choke point.
Fog thickened.
Visibility dropped.
Briggs edged his escort vehicle forward…
Then slowed deliberately.
The van braked.
Donovan mirrored the slowdown behind them.
To outside observers…
Routine traffic adjustment.
To Tate's unit…
Choreography.
"Now," Tate whispered.
Smoke grenades detonated across the roadway.

White clouds erupted, swallowing asphalt and vehicles alike.

Gunfire cracked into the air — controlled, staged, designed to sound chaotic.

Masked officers emerged through the smoke, firing upward and outward to simulate an ambush.

Inside the van, prisoners panicked.

"What's happening?!"

"Stay down!" the driver yelled.

Maya flinched at the first shot but forced herself steady.

Her camera captured everything.

Every muzzle flash.

Every masked officer.

Every staged movement.

"Amina?" she whispered.

"Jamming now."

Amina hit the key.

Encrypted police channels flooded with static.

Inside the escort vehicles, officers tapped their earpieces in confusion.

"Channel interference."

"Switch to secondary."

But switching took time.

And sixty seconds in a live operation was an eternity.

***

On the ridge, a contractor touched his headset.

"We lost comms."

No response.

He hesitated.

Something felt off.

He raised his rifle anyway.

***

Down in the smoke…

Silk stepped into the roadway.

Slow.

Calm.

Unarmed in appearance.

But deadly in intention.

He disappeared into the white cloud like a ghost re-entering the living world.

Briggs moved toward the van door, weapon raised, ready to "neutralize" the prisoners.

He never saw Silk behind him.

An arm wrapped around Briggs' throat.

Fast.

Silent.

Efficient.

Briggs gasped as Silk dragged him into the thicker smoke.

"What the—"

"Not today," Silk whispered.

He slammed Briggs' head against the van panel.

The officer dropped to one knee.

Malik and Rico emerged from the fog instantly, disarming him and pulling him down.

"Got him," Rico muttered.

Dre's voice hit their comms.

"You got thirty seconds before jam breaks. Move!"

***

More figures moved through the haze now — not part of Tate's script.

Contractors spotted motion that wasn't choreographed.

"Unidentified actors in the smoke," one said. "Confirm engagement?"

No answer.

Static.

He aimed anyway.

Maya zoomed tighter through her lens.

Her camera caught a split-second frame of Silk turning his head toward the van…

Face visible.

Eyes burning through the fog.

She didn't know it yet…

…but that frame would matter more than anything she captured that day.

***

Inside Tate's vehicle, the jamming cut out.

Comms snapped back alive.

"What's happening?" Tate demanded.

Marquez answered first.

"Unknown interference. Multiple actors in the smoke. This isn't clean."

Tate's jaw tightened.

He looked through the windshield into the fog.

And realized…

His plan was unraveling.

Fast.

Chapter Nine

The smoke turned the world gray.

Gunshots cracked through the fog like lightning without thunder — sharp bursts tearing holes in visibility, echoing off asphalt and hillside brush.

Everything smelled like burning rubber, gunpowder, and hot metal.

Maya crouched low behind the retaining wall, camera locked in both hands.

Her heart pounded so violently she thought it might shake the lens.

"Keep recording!" Amina shouted beside her, voice tight but steady.

Maya forced her breathing slower.

Forced her hands still.

Through the haze, figures moved in violent fragments.

Masked officers firing upward.

Contractors repositioning on the ridge.

Shadows dragging bodies out of sight.

And in the center of it all…

Silk.

He moved through the smoke like he could see invisible pathways — slipping between gunfire, disrupting formations, pulling officers out of position before they even realized they were exposed.

Malik and Rico sprinted toward the transport van, staying low, using the fog as cover.

Dre's voice cut through their comms.

"You got less than twenty seconds before contractor engagement. Move!"

They reached Briggs' unconscious body and shoved him behind the wheel well.

Rico grabbed his weapon.

Malik scanned the smoke.

"This going sideways fast," he muttered.

"You think?" Rico replied.

***

Inside the escort vehicle, Officer Donovan stumbled out into the haze, coughing hard.

His weapon was drawn…

…but his hands shook.

He saw masked officers firing staged shots.

Saw contractors aiming into the fog without clear targets.

Saw prisoners inside the van screaming in confusion.

None of this looked like procedure anymore.

This looked like slaughter waiting for permission.

He turned slowly…

And saw Silk stepping toward him through the smoke.

Time froze.

Recognition hit Donovan like a punch to the chest.

The raid.

The apartment doorway.

Silk's brother on the floor in cuffs.

Tate planting evidence.

Donovan saying nothing.

Silk stopped ten feet away.

His voice was calm.

Too calm for the battlefield around them.

"You."

Donovan swallowed hard.

"Silk… listen—"

"You were there," Silk said quietly. "When Tate framed my brother."

Donovan shook his head violently.

"I didn't know what he was doing. I swear I didn't."

"You watched," Silk replied.

Gunfire cracked somewhere behind them.

Donovan lowered his weapon slightly.

"I was new. I didn't have rank. I didn't have power—"

"You had a voice," Silk cut in. "And you buried it."

The words hit harder than any bullet.

Donovan's breath hitched.

Smoke thickened around them like the city itself was holding the moment still.

"You don't have to keep choosing him," Silk said. "You can stop right now."

Donovan glanced toward the convoy…

Toward Tate's silhouette through the fog.

"I can't," he whispered. "Nobody just walks away from Tate."

"That ain't loyalty," Silk said.

"That's fear."

Donovan didn't deny it.

***

A shout tore through the smoke.

"DONOVAN — DOWN!"

Tate's voice.

Sharp.

Commanding.

Silk turned instinctively toward the sound.

And Tate fired.

The shot cracked clean through the fog.

The bullet grazed Silk's shoulder, spinning him sideways.

He dropped to one knee, blood blooming dark across his hoodie.

Maya gasped behind the wall.

Her camera zoomed hard on the moment — Tate firing… Silk falling… Donovan frozen between them.

Malik's voice erupted through comms.

"SILK!"

He and Rico sprinted toward him, dragging him back into cover.

Silk clenched his teeth but didn't cry out.

Pain was familiar.

Pain wasn't new.

***

Donovan stared at Tate in disbelief.

"You shot him?" he shouted.

Tate reloaded calmly, unfazed.

"He's a criminal," Tate replied. "You hesitate again, Donovan, and you get the same."

Something inside Donovan snapped.

Years of silence.

Years of looking away.

Years of swallowing wrong.

"No," Donovan said quietly.

Then louder:

"Not this time."

He raised his weapon…

Not at Silk.

At Tate.

The world went still.

Even the contractors hesitated.

Tate's eyes hardened into something cold enough to freeze blood.

"You point that at me," Tate said slowly, "you better pull the trigger."

Donovan's hands trembled…

…but he didn't lower the gun.

Behind him, prisoners were being pulled from the van by masked counter-attackers.

The fake ambush had turned real.

Tate looked past Donovan toward the escaping inmates.

"You really choosing them over your badge?" Tate asked.

Donovan's voice cracked.

"I'm choosing what's right."

Tate smirked faintly.

"Right don't exist out here," he said. "Only survival."

Gunfire erupted again on the ridge — contractors firing warning shots as they repositioned.

Dre's voice burst through comms.

"Time's up! Contractors engaging! Everybody disengage now!"

Malik and Rico lifted Silk between them, retreating into smoke cover.

Maya kept filming — every second, every betrayal, every truth.

Donovan slowly stepped backward, weapon still aimed at Tate.

He didn't run.

But he didn't stand beside Tate anymore either.

That line had been crossed.

And it could never be uncrossed.

***

Minutes later…

The smoke thinned.

The convoy was wrecked.

Glass littered the asphalt.

The van doors hung open.

The prisoners were gone.

Alive.

Free.

Tate stood in the middle of the road, breathing slow, watching the chaos settle.

His plan hadn't just failed.

It had been exposed.

And somewhere inside that exposure…

War had officially begun.

Chapter Ten

When the shooting finally stopped, morning had already broken.

Sunlight cut through the thinning smoke in pale gold streaks, turning the wrecked roadway into something surreal — like the aftermath of a nightmare refusing to end.

The convoy was destroyed.

Escort vehicles sat crooked, windshields shattered.

Shell casings glittered across the asphalt like broken glass confetti.

The transport van's rear doors hung open, swaying slowly in the breeze.

Inside…

Empty shackles.

The prisoners were gone.

Alive.

Hidden.

For now.

Dre moved through the scene with quiet precision, directing the final retreat like a man who had done this long before today.

"Move him," he said, nodding toward Silk.

Malik and Rico lifted Silk carefully, each holding one side as they guided him up the slope away from the road.

Silk gritted his teeth but didn't complain.

Pain didn't scare him.

Exposure did.

Maya jogged beside them, camera still running out of instinct more than decision.

"We need to get you to Highland," she said breathlessly.

Silk shot her a sideways look.

"You think I walk into a hospital with a bullet wound and walk back out?" he asked.

She hesitated.

"Then where?"

"The rec center," he said. "Patch it there."

He tried to stand on his own.

His knees buckled.

Malik tightened his grip.

"Don't be stubborn right now," he said.

Silk exhaled through clenched teeth.

"Stubborn kept me alive this long."

Rico smirked slightly.

"Yeah, well today teamwork did."

They kept moving.

Behind them, Dre scanned the roadway one last time — ensuring no one had been left behind, no evidence abandoned that could trace back to them.

Only then did he retreat into the brush.

The ambush was over.

But the consequences had just begun.

***

By noon, the first lie hit the airwaves.

Every major Bay Area news outlet carried the same breaking headline:

GANG-LED PRISONER BREAKOUT ATTEMPT

TWO INMATES DEAD — MULTIPLE OFFICERS INJURED

Maya stared at the TV in disbelief.

They had gathered back inside the rec center, now transformed from staging ground into recovery shelter.

Silk sat shirtless in a folding chair while DeShawn stitched the graze wound in his shoulder.

He barely flinched.

But Maya couldn't pull her eyes from the screen.

"This is wrong," she whispered.

Amina typed furiously on her laptop beside her.

"They're using Tate's narrative already," she said. "Even before official reports filed."

On screen, traffic cam footage rolled.

Blurry figures.

Smoke.

Gunfire.

A masked silhouette near the van.

The anchor's voice filled the room:

"Authorities believe the attack was coordinated by a violent East Oakland gang seeking to free incarcerated members."

Rico scoffed loudly.

"Violent gang? We stopped a massacre."

Malik paced the room, fists clenched.

"They flipped the whole story."

Dre stood silent, watching the broadcast like a man studying enemy propaganda.

"They're moving fast," he said. "Means this narrative was prewritten."

Maya felt her stomach twist.

Of course it was.

Tate didn't plan operations without planning aftermaths.

The footage shifted again.

A freeze-frame image appeared.

One of the masked "ambushers."

But the mask had slipped slightly…

Revealing OPD tactical gear beneath.

Maya's eyes widened.

"They aired that?" she asked.

Amina zoomed the image on her laptop.

"Low resolution. Grainy. They betting nobody notices."

Maya reached into her bag and pulled out her camera.

"I got clearer footage," she said.

Everyone looked at her.

"How clear?" Dre asked.

She powered the device on and scrolled to the clip.

Paused it.

Zoomed.

There — unmistakable — Tate firing through the smoke.

Silk falling.

Donovan aiming back at Tate.

The room went silent.

Amina whispered:

"This could blow the whole thing open."

Dre nodded slowly.

"Or get us all killed if released wrong."

Silk spoke up from the chair, voice calm despite the blood loss.

"You don't leak it to the news first," he said.

"Why not?" Malik asked.

"Because the news already owned," Silk replied. "You release it public direct. No middleman."

Amina nodded.

"Encrypted drop. Multiple platforms. Mirror uploads so it can't be scrubbed."

Maya looked between them all.

She hadn't asked for this role.

But the city had chosen her.

Her voice.

Her lens.

Her truth.

She swallowed hard.

"Then we expose it," she said.

Dre studied her for a moment — measuring resolve.

Then nodded.

"Then we do it smart."

***

Across town, inside a private conference room at OPD head-quarters…

Tate stood at the head of the table watching the same news coverage play across a mounted screen.

Other officers sat around him.

City legal advisors.

A man in a tailored suit nobody introduced.

"The narrative is holding," the suited man said calmly.

Tate nodded.

"And the escaped prisoners?"

"Recovery teams are tracking," the man replied. "But that's secondary."

Tate glanced at him.

"Secondary?"

The man folded his hands.

"What matters now is maintaining public perception. The East must look unstable."

Tate understood immediately.

This was never just revenge.

It was strategy.

Urban cleansing disguised as crisis response.

"Press conference at four," the man continued. "You'll lead it."

Tate smirked faintly.

"Of course I will."

As the screen replayed the "gang ambush" headline, Tate leaned back in his chair, confident again.

He believed he had already won the story.

What he didn't know…

Was that the real footage was sitting inside a broken rec center…

Waiting to change everything.

Chapter Eleven

The rec center smelled like antiseptic and anxiety.

The same gym that had echoed with training drills two nights ago now felt like an underground newsroom — wires running across the floor, laptops glowing in the dim light, voices low but urgent.

Outside, Oakland moved through its day unaware that truth was being sharpened inside a boarded-up building on 47th.

Silk sat shirtless at the folding table, shoulder freshly bandaged.

The bullet graze had been shallow, but it burned every time he moved.

He didn't complain.

Pain wasn't the problem.

Timing was.

"You need to stay still," DeShawn said, tightening the wrap.

Silk smirked faintly.

"I been still long enough in life."

Across the room, Maya and Amina sat shoulder to shoulder, both staring at the same footage playing frame by frame on Amina's screen.

Maya's camera footage.

Uncut.

Unfiltered.

Unspun.

The truth.

She watched again as Tate fired through the smoke.

Watched Silk fall.

Watched Donovan raise his weapon back at his own commanding officer.

Her chest tightened.

"This changes everything," she whispered.

Amina didn't answer right away.

She zoomed in on the frame, isolating badge numbers, tactical gear identifiers, vehicle plates partially visible through smoke.

"It could," Amina said finally.

"But only if it reaches the public before OPD buries it."

Malik paced behind them, restless energy spilling out of every step.

"How long to upload?" he asked.

Amina shook her head.

"Uploading is easy. Surviving the upload is hard."

He frowned.

"What that mean?"

She turned toward him.

"Once this goes live, we not just witnesses anymore. We targets."

Silence settled over the room.

No one argued that.

They all understood what exposure meant.

Dre stepped forward, placing a printed map beside the laptops.

"We stagger the release," he said. "Multiple encrypted plat-forms. Offshore servers. Anonymous drops."

Amina nodded.

"I already got mirror sites prepped. Once it's out, scrubbing it becomes impossible."

Maya swallowed.

Her hands hovered over the keyboard.

"You ready?" Amina asked her.

Maya hesitated.

Then nodded slowly.

"Yeah."

But inside…

She knew once she hit upload, there was no going back to being just a poet.

She would become evidence.

***

Across town, Donovan sat alone in his apartment, TV muted but flashing the same headlines on loop.

GANG-LED BREAKOUT ATTEMPT

OFFICERS HEROICALLY RESPOND

He stared at the screen like it might confess something if he looked long enough.

His uniform hung over the back of a chair.

Untouched since the ambush.

His phone buzzed.

Unknown number.

He hesitated…

Then answered.

No one spoke at first.

Then a voice came through — low, distorted.

"You pointed a weapon at your commanding officer today."

Donovan's spine stiffened.

"Who is this?"

"You know who this is," the voice replied calmly.

Tate.

"Where are you?" Donovan asked.

"Where you should've stayed," Tate said. "Behind me."

Donovan clenched his jaw.

"You shot an unarmed man."

"I neutralized a threat," Tate corrected. "And you hesitated."

"He wasn't the threat," Donovan said quietly.

Silence crackled through the line.

Then Tate spoke again, colder.

"You need to decide what side of this you're on, son."

"I already did," Donovan replied.

The call disconnected instantly.

Donovan stared at the dead phone screen, chest rising slowly.

He knew what that call meant.

He wasn't being warned.

He was being marked.

***

Back at the rec center…

Amina finished encoding the footage.

"File split into thirty fragments," she said. "Reassembly key only activates once upload completes."

Dre nodded approvingly.

"Smart."

"Necessary," she replied.

She turned to Maya.

"Whenever you're ready."

Maya stared at the screen.

Her footage timeline stretched across hours of chaos.

Evidence stacked in digital layers.

If she released this…

She wasn't just exposing police corruption.

She was exposing city-level conspiracy.

Her fingers hovered over the key.

Silk's voice came from behind her.

"You scared?"

She nodded.

"Yeah."

"Good," he said quietly. "Means you understand the weight."

She looked up at him.

"What if this makes things worse?"

Silk didn't sugarcoat it.

"It will."

She blinked.

"But worse truth better than peaceful lie," he added.

She inhaled slowly.

Then pressed the key.

UPLOAD INITIATED.

Progress bar crawled forward.

10%.

20%.

No one spoke.

Every second felt like standing in open crosshairs.

50%.

Amina monitored traffic spikes.

"So far we clean."

70%.

Dre scanned the boarded windows instinctively.

90%.

Maya's pulse pounded in her ears.

100%.

UPLOAD COMPLETE.

Amina immediately triggered the mirror releases.

"Distributing now. International nodes… independent journalists… activist networks."

Malik exhaled hard.

"So it's out?"

Amina nodded.

"It's out."

Silk leaned back in his chair.

"Then the war just changed fronts."

***

Forty minutes later…

News alerts exploded across phones citywide.

UNVERIFIED FOOTAGE QUESTIONS OFFICIAL POLICE ACCOUNT

OPD AMBUSH STORY CHALLENGED BY NEW VIDEO EVIDENCE

Maya's footage played across independent media streams — Tate firing… Silk falling… Donovan aiming back.

The narrative cracked open like glass under pressure.

But exposure came with consequences.

Across town…

Donovan's apartment door creaked open.

He hadn't locked it.

Didn't think he needed to.

He stepped inside cautiously.

Something felt wrong.

Too quiet.

Too still.

Then he saw it.

His apartment had been searched.

Drawers open.

Papers scattered.

His service weapon missing from the drawer where he kept it off-duty.

And on his kitchen table…

A single envelope.

No name.

No return address.

Inside…

A printed still frame from Maya's footage.

Donovan aiming his weapon at Tate.

Beneath it, typed in clean black letters:

YOU CHOSE A SIDE.

He stood frozen in the middle of his own apartment…

Realizing he was no longer part of the operation.

He was part of the cleanup.

Chapter Twelve

Oakland woke up angry.

By sunrise, Maya's footage had already spread beyond the Bay.

Independent journalists were dissecting it frame by frame.

Activist accounts reposted slowed-down clips showing badge identifiers under masks.

Hashtags flooded social media:

#OaklandSetup

#BadgeOrGang

#JusticeForTheEast

But alongside the outrage came confusion.

Because for every voice calling the footage proof...

There was another calling it doctored.

Manipulated.

Gang propaganda.

The city wasn't just reacting.

It was splitting.

Inside the rec center, the squad watched the chaos unfold across three separate screens.

News panels argued.

Former officers defended protocol.

Community leaders demanded investigations.

"This is exactly what they want," Dre said quietly.

Maya looked at him.

"What do you mean?"

"They don't mind truth leaking," he replied. "They just muddy it until nobody knows what to believe."

Silk sat nearby, shoulder stiff but healing.

"That confusion buys them time," he added.

Amina scrolled through encrypted feeds.

"They're already pushing counter-narratives," she said. "Calling the footage 'selectively edited.'"

Maya shook her head.

"It's uncut."

"Doesn't matter," Amina replied. "Truth don't spread faster than doubt."

On screen, a BREAKING NEWS banner appeared.

OPD PRESS CONFERENCE — LIVE

Dre muted the room instantly.

The broadcast cut to a podium outside police headquarters.

Sergeant Marcus Tate stepped into frame in full dress uniform.

Calm.

Collected.

Untouched by scandal.

Maya's stomach tightened just seeing him.

Tate adjusted the mic.

"Good afternoon," he began.

"First, I want to assure the public that the Oakland Police Department remains fully committed to the safety of this city."

He paused — measured, controlled.

"Regarding the footage circulating online... we have reason to believe it has been manipulated to misrepresent officer response during a violent gang-led ambush."

Malik cursed under his breath.

"Manipulated?"

Tate continued smoothly:

"Our officers were responding to an attempted prisoner extraction orchestrated by organized criminal elements. Any force used was in defense of life and public safety."

Maya felt her fists clench.

"He's lying," she whispered.

Silk didn't take his eyes off the screen.

"He ain't lying," he said.

"He's rewriting."

Tate finished with a promise of "internal review," then stepped away from the podium like a man confident the room still belonged to him.

The media ate it up.

Some questioned.

Some nodded.

But doubt had been planted.

And doubt was enough.

***

That same afternoon…

The retaliation began.

Unmarked police vehicles rolled through East Oakland in patterns that didn't match patrol routes.

Surveillance units parked near rec centers, churches, barber shops.

Drones buzzed faintly over rooftops.

They weren't investigating.

They were mapping.

Amina tracked it all from her laptop.

"They activated urban monitoring grids," she said. "License plate sweeps. Facial recognition. Cell tower triangulation."

Malik frowned.

"You saying they hunting us?"

"I'm saying," she replied, "they building cases before making arrests."

Dre stood at the window, watching a black SUV idle two blocks down.

"They not coming fast," he said.

"They coming thorough."
***
Across town…

Donovan sat in his darkened apartment, watching Tate's press conference replay on mute.

He hadn't slept.

Hadn't changed clothes.

The envelope on his table still sat open.

YOU CHOSE A SIDE.

His phone buzzed again.

This time — an internal department alert.

MANDATORY DEBRIEF — ALL ESCORT PERSONNEL — 18:00 HOURS

He stared at the message.

He knew what it really meant.

Interrogation.

Control.

Containment.

He grabbed his jacket slowly.

If he went…

He might never leave that room clean.

If he didn't…

He'd be marked openly.

He glanced at the printed still frame again — him aiming at Tate.

His reflection stared back from the dark TV screen.

He whispered to himself:

"What did I just step into…"
***
Back at the rec center…

Night fell heavier than usual.

No one left.

No one trusted the streets enough to walk them alone now.

Maya sat on the gym floor reviewing footage backups.

For the first time, fear crept in not from the violence…

But from visibility.

She had put her face behind the truth.
And truth made enemies.
Silk approached quietly.
"You did good," he said.
She didn't look up.
"Did I?"
He sat beside her.
"You cracked their armor," he said. "They just pretending it ain't dented."
She nodded slowly.
"But armor cracks mean retaliation too."
He didn't deny it.
Outside, a helicopter passed low over the neighborhood.
Its spotlight cut across rooftops like a searchlight hunting ghosts.
Maya looked up at it.
Then back at her footage.
The fight had changed.
The battlefield had expanded.
And the city…
The city was officially watching them now.

Chapter Thirteen

The first sign that things had changed wasn't loud.

It was quiet.

Too quiet.

Maya noticed it when she left the rec center just before noon to grab fresh batteries and storage drives from her apartment.

The streets looked normal.

Traffic moved.

Corner stores buzzed.

Kids walked home from school.

But the rhythm felt… staged.

Like background actors hitting marks.

She turned onto her block and saw the black sedan parked across the street from her building.

Engine off.

Windows tinted.

No one inside that she could see.

But she felt watched.

She told herself she was being paranoid.

Until she reached her apartment door.

The lock wasn't broken.

But it wasn't sitting right either.

A millimeter off alignment.

Enough that someone careful would notice.

Her chest tightened.

She pushed the door open slowly.

Nothing looked trashed.

Nothing overturned.

But things were wrong.

Subtle wrong.

Her bookshelf had shifted slightly.

Her notebook stack had been touched.

Her camera case was unzipped.

Whoever had been there…

Wasn't looking for valuables.

They were looking for evidence.

Her footage backups.

Her breath shortened.

She moved quickly to the closet and pulled out the hidden drive she had taped inside an old shoe box.

Still there.

Still intact.

But now she knew.

They knew about her.

She grabbed the drive, stuffed it in her hoodie pocket, and left immediately without grabbing anything else.

By the time she reached the street again…

The black sedan was gone.

***

Back at the rec center, Maya burst through the doors.

"They've been in my apartment," she said.

The room went still.

Silk looked up first.

"Police?"

"I don't know," she replied. "But they weren't stealing. They were searching."

Amina closed her laptop halfway.

"That means they're tracing the leak source."

Dre's expression darkened.

"They moving faster than expected."

Malik stepped closer to Maya.

"You good?"

She nodded, but her hands shook.

"They know it was me."

Silk stood slowly.

"No," he said. "They suspect it's you. Big difference."

"How comforting," she muttered.

Dre grabbed a marker and walked to the map wall.

"If they surveilling Maya, they surveilling all of us," he said.

Amina nodded.

"I'm already seeing cell tower pings increasing around this block."

Rico exhaled sharply.

"So we on a clock now."

"Been on one," Silk said. "Now it just louder."

***

Across town…

Donovan never made it to his debrief.

The police station logged his absence immediately.

Within an hour, an internal alert went out:

OFFICER DONOVAN — UNACCOUNTED FOR

Tate read the alert in silence from his office desk.

He didn't look surprised.

He looked irritated.

"He ran," Briggs said from across the room.

Tate shook his head slightly.

"No," he said. "He didn't run."

Briggs frowned.

"Then where is he?"

Tate leaned back slowly.

"He's thinking."

Briggs didn't like the sound of that.

"What you want done?"

Tate didn't hesitate.

"Find him before someone else does."

***

That evening, Dre gathered the crew again.

Tension had thickened inside the rec center.

Nobody sat casually anymore.

Nobody relaxed.

Dre spoke first.

"They searching apartments now. Quiet warrants. Digital tracing. Informant sweeps."

Amina added:

"They're also scrubbing social platforms trying to flag original upload nodes."

Maya crossed her arms.

"So we stirred the hornet's nest."

Silk shook his head.

"Nah," he said. "We kicked the hive open."

He stepped toward the map.

"But this ain't just police retaliation," he continued.

He tapped redevelopment zones highlighted in red.

"These neighborhoods? Already approved for infrastructure expansion."

Malik frowned.

"What that got to do with this?"

Silk looked at him.

"Everything."

Dre nodded slowly.

"The ambush was phase one," he said.

"Destabilize the East. Justify heavy enforcement. Push residents out."

Amina zoomed satellite overlays onto her laptop.

"Property acquisition filings increased 300% last quarter," she said.

Maya felt sick.

"So they planning displacement using violence as justification."

Silk met her eyes.

"Urban cleansing dressed up as public safety."
The room fell silent.
Because now…
This wasn't just about prisoners anymore.
It wasn't even just about corruption.
It was about land.
Control.
Erasure.
***
Later that night…
Maya sat alone on the rec center rooftop.
Her camera rested beside her.
For the first time since this started…
She wasn't filming.
She was thinking.
Silk climbed up quietly and sat beside her.
"You realizing it bigger than you thought?" he asked.
She nodded slowly.
"I thought I was exposing one operation."
"You exposed a system," he said.
She exhaled.
"They searched my home."
He didn't look surprised.
"That means you matter now."
She looked at him.
"I don't know if I wanted to matter like this."
He gave a faint smirk.
"Nobody do."
A helicopter passed low overhead, spotlight sweeping rooftops.
She watched it fade into the night sky.
"I'm not just documenting anymore," she said quietly.
Silk shook his head.
"No," he said.
"You part of the fight now."
She picked up her camera again.
Held it tighter this time.

Fear still lived in her chest.

But so did resolve.

And beneath Oakland's skyline…

The war that started on asphalt had now spread into homes, networks, and city hall itself.

There was no going back to normal.

Not for her.

Not for any of them.

Chapter Fourteen

The city didn't announce the crackdown.

It just started happening.

Quiet at first.

Unmarked vehicles posted at corners that didn't need watching.

Drones hovering low over rooftops under the excuse of "traffic monitoring."

Extra patrol units cruising blocks they had ignored for years.

But the people of East Oakland noticed.

They always did.

Because when the police showed up in numbers like this…

It never meant protection.

It meant pressure.

***

Maya saw it firsthand walking back from the corner store that morning.

Two officers stood outside Mrs. Li's herbal shop asking questions.

Not loud.

Not aggressive.

But invasive.

Mrs. Li's answers were short, polite — but her eyes flicked constantly toward the street like she didn't trust who might be listening.

Maya slowed her pace as she passed.

One of the officers glanced at her too long.

Not recognizing…

But cataloging.

She kept walking without making eye contact.

Her pulse ticked up anyway.

Everywhere she looked, the city felt watched.

Not guarded.

Watched.

***

Back at the rec center, Amina had already mapped the expansion.

She projected a digital grid across the wall using a portable display unit.

Colored markers blinked across East Oakland like infection points.

"Mobile surveillance units increased forty percent overnight," she said.

Dre studied the map.

"They not searching randomly," he said. "They triangulating."

Amina zoomed in.

"Cell tower sweeps, license plate recognition, facial capture at intersections."

Malik frowned.

"You saying they building a net?"

Silk answered before Amina could.

"Nah," he said quietly.

"They closing one."

Everyone looked at him.

He continued:

"They already picked targets. Now they tightening circles until they reach 'em."

Rico cracked his knuckles.

"So when do they start snatching people?"

Silk didn't sugarcoat it.

"They already have."

***

The first raid hit that afternoon.

Not on gang members.

Not on criminals.

On a community center two blocks from Foothill — one known for hosting tenant rights meetings and youth workshops.

Police stormed it under warrant of "organized gang affiliation."

Doors kicked in.

Computers seized.

Volunteers detained for questioning.

News cameras showed up just in time to capture the spectacle — not the aftermath.

Maya watched the coverage in silence.

"They not even hiding it now," she said.

Dre nodded.

"They creating visual justification. Make enforcement look necessary."

Amina tapped her keyboard.

"They also seized three external hard drives from the center."

Maya's stomach tightened.

"Looking for more footage."

"Or proof of coordination," Amina said.

Silk leaned against the wall, arms crossed.

"They want to paint the East like a coordinated insurgency."

Malik shook his head.

"All this because we exposed one operation?"

Silk's eyes hardened.

"No," he said.

"All this because exposure makes their long-term plans harder."

He stepped toward the map.

"Fear pushes residents out faster than eviction notices."

Maya looked at the blinking grid again.

"They're weaponizing perception."

Dre nodded.

"Always been the strategy."

***

That evening, helicopters circled lower than usual.

Spotlights dragged across rooftops like search fingers.

People stayed indoors.

Porch conversations disappeared.

Even music played quieter.

The neighborhood felt occupied without tanks ever rolling in.

On the west side of the city...

Silk made a call.

He stood alone beside an abandoned warehouse near the port, phone pressed to his ear.

A voice answered on the second ring.

"Thought you disappeared, Silk."

"Still here," he replied.

"What you need?"

Silk looked out toward the cranes lining the harbor skyline.

"East heating up. Police pushing heavy."

The voice on the line sighed.

"We been seeing it from this side too."

Silk's tone lowered.

"I might need West Oakland to stand ready."

A pause.

Then:

"You calling favors now?"

"I'm calling solidarity."

Another pause.

Then the voice replied:

"If East bleed... West bleed too."

Silk ended the call without another word.

Because he knew what that meant.

Reinforcements.

Community protection networks.

Street organizations aligning under one defensive cause.

The city thought it was isolating the East.

Instead…
It was waking the West.
***
Back at the rec center, Maya reviewed new footage she'd captured earlier that day — patrol saturation, drone paths, officer clustering patterns.
Her role had evolved.
She wasn't just documenting events anymore.
She was mapping state behavior.
Amina leaned over her shoulder.
"You're building intelligence profiles," she said.
Maya nodded.
"Information keeps people alive."
Silk walked in just then.
"Or gets them killed faster if leaked wrong."
Maya didn't flinch at the warning.
"I know."
He studied her for a moment.
"You different than when this started."
She looked up at him.
"How?"
"You don't look scared anymore."
She thought about that.
Then answered honestly:
"I'm still scared."
She paused.
"But fear ain't stopping me now."
Silk nodded slowly.
"That's when people become dangerous."
Outside, another helicopter cut across the skyline.
Its spotlight grazed the rec center roof briefly before moving on.
But the message was clear.
The city was closing in.
And the deeper the truth spread…
The tighter the surveillance net would pull.

Chapter Fifteen

Donovan knew the moment he stepped into the precinct parking structure that something was wrong.

Too many unmarked vehicles.

Too many officers lingering instead of moving.

Too many eyes watching instead of working.

He parked slowly, scanning reflections in the concrete pillars before stepping out.

No one approached him.

But that silence was louder than confrontation.

He walked into the building anyway.

Because not showing up would've made him guilty.

Showing up just made him vulnerable.

Inside, the atmosphere felt staged.

Conversations stopped when he passed.

Officers who once joked with him now avoided eye contact.

Others watched him openly.

Not as a colleague.

As a liability.

"Officer Donovan."

He turned.

Two Internal Affairs investigators stood behind him — suits, badges, neutral expressions polished to intimidation.

"We need you in conference room three."

He didn't ask why.

He already knew.

***

The conference room lights felt too bright.

A recorder sat in the center of the table already running.

Tate stood at the far wall.

Silent.

Observing.

Not participating.

Just watching like a man studying a suspect instead of a subordinate.

Donovan sat down slowly.

Internal Affairs began immediately.

"Officer Donovan, walk us through your actions during the prisoner transport incident."

He exhaled.

"I followed escort protocol until the ambush."

"Ambush by who?" the investigator pressed.

"Unknown actors."

Tate smirked faintly behind them.

Donovan noticed.

His jaw tightened.

"Did you discharge your weapon?"

"No."

"Why not?"

"Visibility was compromised."

"Or hesitation?" the second investigator asked.

Donovan stayed silent.

They slid a printed still frame across the table.

Maya's footage.

Him aiming at Tate.

His chest tightened.

"Explain this."

He stared at the image.

Then looked up.

"I believed a civilian was being wrongfully engaged."

Tate stepped forward for the first time.

"You believed?" he said quietly.

Donovan met his eyes.

"I saw you shoot an unarmed man."

The room went still.

Internal Affairs glanced between them.

Tate spoke calmly.

"That 'unarmed man' is a known gang lieutenant tied to multiple violent offenses."

"He wasn't a threat in that moment," Donovan said.

Tate leaned closer.

"You hesitated in a live operation," he replied. "That hesitation endangered officers."

Donovan didn't back down.

"What endangered officers was staging an execution."

The investigators stiffened slightly.

The recorder kept running.

Tate studied him for a long moment.

Then smiled faintly.

"We'll conclude the debrief here."

He turned to Internal Affairs.

"Officer Donovan is suspended pending review."

Donovan didn't react outwardly.

But inside…

The line had been crossed permanently.

He stood and walked out without another word.

***

By the time he reached his car…

Two black SUVs pulled into the structure entrance simultaneously.

Unmarked.

Government plates.

He froze halfway to the driver's door.

Not police.

Not officially.

Recovery teams.

Silk's warning echoed in his mind.

Nobody walks away from Tate.

He moved fast — abandoning the car, slipping into the stairwell instead.

Footsteps echoed behind him almost instantly.

They had been waiting.

He pushed through the stairwell exit onto a side street and didn't stop running until he reached the BART platform two blocks away.

He boarded the first train without checking the destination.

He just needed distance.

Time.

Air.

As the train pulled away from downtown Oakland…

He realized something heavy:

He wasn't suspended.

He was being erased.

***

That night…

Silk got the call.

He stood outside the rec center, phone to his ear, listening quietly.

"Donovan didn't show up to IA follow-up," the voice on the line said.

Silk didn't look surprised.

"Where he at now?"

"Off grid. Left precinct on foot. Surveillance lost him near 12th Street BART."

Silk ended the call and walked inside.

The crew looked up immediately.

"What's wrong?" Maya asked.

Silk spoke plainly.

"Donovan missing."

Malik frowned.

"Missing like kidnapped… or missing like hiding?"

"Both possible," Silk replied.

Dre folded his arms.

"If Tate think Donovan a liability, he'll either silence him… or frame him."

Amina pulled up transit camera feeds.

"Last sighting was underground rail. No exit capture yet."

Maya looked between them.

"So what do we do?"

Silk didn't hesitate.

"We find him before Tate does."

Malik scoffed slightly.

"We really risking ourselves for a cop?"

Silk met his eyes.

"He ain't just a cop anymore," he said.

"He a witness."

Dre nodded slowly.

"And witnesses don't live long in conspiracies like this."

The room fell quiet again.

Because now the war had crossed another threshold.

They weren't just fighting to expose truth.

They were racing to protect it…

Before it disappeared forever.

Chapter Sixteen

West Oakland didn't move the same way the East did.

The East reacted loud — protests, gatherings, visible anger.

The West...

Moved quieter.

More deliberate.

More organized.

So when Silk crossed the Mandela Parkway overpass just after midnight, he already knew the call he made earlier had traveled faster than phones.

Word-of-mouth in West Oakland moved like electricity through steel.

He pulled up outside an abandoned shipping warehouse near the port — the kind of place nobody questioned activity after dark.

Floodlights glowed inside.

Engines idled outside.

He stepped out of the car and walked toward the open loading doors.

Inside...

Dozens of men and women stood in clusters.

Not gangs tonight.

Neighborhood protectors.

Dock workers.

Former street soldiers.

Community organizers.

Old heads and young energy in the same room.

The air felt serious, not chaotic.

At the center stood Marcus "Reign" Holloway — tall, gray-bearded, eyes sharp enough to cut through lies before they formed.

He and Silk locked eyes immediately.

"You took your time getting here," Reign said.

Silk smirked faintly.

"Had to make sure East was still standing."

Reign nodded once.

"We been watching."

Silk stepped deeper inside.

"You saw the footage?"

"Everybody saw it," Reign replied. "Police staging executions… contractors in city limits… that ain't law enforcement. That's occupation."

Silk leaned against a crate.

"They escalating surveillance too. Raids starting. Community centers first."

Reign didn't look surprised.

"Testing fear response."

Silk nodded.

"They trying to isolate the East."

Reign stepped closer.

"Then they miscalculated."

Silk raised an eyebrow.

"How so?"

Reign gestured around the warehouse.

"Because West Oakland don't watch neighbors bleed quietly."

Murmurs of agreement rippled through the room.

One woman stepped forward — Lena Torres, community defense organizer, former Army medic turned neighborhood responder.

"We already set up patrol rotations," she said. "Unarmed observation teams. Documenting police movement."

Another man added:

"Safe houses too. If folks need to disappear short-term."

Silk took it in.

This wasn't gang mobilization.

This was community infrastructure activating under pressure.

Still…

He glanced toward Reign.

"You sure this don't turn into open war?"

Reign's expression hardened slightly.

"Depends on how far the city push."

***

Back in East Oakland, Dre listened as Silk relayed the meeting details.

He didn't look relieved.

He looked concerned.

"You pulling West into this changes scale," Dre said.

Silk nodded.

"That's the point."

Dre shook his head slightly.

"More people involved means more people at risk."

"People already at risk," Silk replied.

Maya watched the exchange quietly.

There was tension there — not hostility, but difference in philosophy.

Dre thought defensively.

Contain the threat.

Silk thought collectively.

Expand resistance.

Malik leaned forward.

"So West really standing with us?"

Silk nodded.

"Patrol networks already forming. Surveillance counter-watching police."

Amina perked up.

"That could help with drone tracking."

Silk looked at her.

"They also got signal disruptors from port contacts."

She blinked.

"Okay… I like the West."

Even Dre cracked a faint smile at that.

***

Two nights later…

Joint patrols began quietly.

Unarmed observers positioned at rooftops, intersections, transit hubs.

Not interfering.

Just watching the watchers.

Police vehicles slowed when they realized they were being documented back.

Drones pulled higher to avoid handheld tracking lasers activists deployed.

The city's surveillance net was now being studied from the ground up.

And word spread fast:

East and West were unified.

***

On the rec center rooftop, Maya filmed the skyline again — but this time from a different emotional place.

Not fear.

Awareness.

She captured footage of patrol caravans moving between neighborhoods — headlights gliding like veins of light through the city.

Silk joined her, leaning against the ledge.

"You seeing it now?" he asked.

"Seeing what?"

He gestured toward the lights below.

"How communities move when systems fail."

She nodded slowly.

"It's bigger than the ambush now."

He smiled faintly.

"Been bigger."

She lowered the camera.

"So what happens if the city escalates again?"

Silk didn't hesitate.

"Then the West don't just watch."

She looked at him.

"And you?"

He met her eyes directly.

"I stop thinking like a neighborhood lieutenant…"

"…and start thinking like a general."

She believed him.

Because something about the way West Oakland mobilized…

Felt less like reaction…

And more like preparation.

***

Across town…

In a private city planning office overlooking downtown Oakland…

The suited man who had stood beside Tate during the press conference reviewed surveillance reports on a tablet.

He spoke without looking up.

"Community mobilization spreading westward."

Another official nodded nervously.

"Yes sir. Joint patrols forming."

The man sighed slightly.

"Containment window is closing."

He turned the tablet toward Tate, who stood nearby.

"Accelerate phase two."

Tate didn't ask questions.

He already knew what that meant.

More raids.

More arrests.

More pressure.
Because when communities unified…
The city didn't negotiate.
It crushed.
And the next wave of retaliation…
Was already being prepared.

Chapter Seventeen

The raids started at 4:12 a.m.

Not random. Not scattered. Coordinated. Simultaneous strikes across East Oakland — twenty locations hit within the same thirty-minute window.

Doors kicked in before sunrise.

Flashlights tore through living rooms like interrogation beams.

People dragged from beds without explanation.

No warrants shown.

No charges announced.

Just force.

***

Maya woke to her phone vibrating violently against the metal folding table beside her.

Amina's name flashed across the screen.

She answered immediately.

"It's happening," Amina said, voice tight.

"What's happening?"

"Raids. Multiple. Community leaders, organizers, even volunteers from the center that got hit last week."

Maya sat up fast.

"They arresting them?"

"Detaining," Amina said. "But they calling it 'gang coordination sweeps.'"

Maya's stomach dropped.

Media narrative construction in real time.

She grabbed her camera instinctively.

"I'm filming this."

"Be careful," Amina warned. "They expanding surveillance too."

Maya was already moving.

***

Outside, the neighborhood looked like a war zone staged for cameras.

Police lights painted houses red and blue.

Armored vehicles blocked intersections.

Neighbors stood on sidewalks in pajamas, filming with phones while officers barked orders to disperse.

Maya filmed everything.

A grandmother pushed against a patrol line screaming about her grandson being taken without cause.

A youth counselor zip-tied on his own porch.

Volunteers from the rec center face-down on concrete.

None resisting.

Still treated like combatants.

Her camera shook — not from fear…

From anger.

***

Across town…

West Oakland patrol units mobilized immediately.

Word traveled fast through community channels.

Observation teams repositioned at intersections where East residents were being transported.

Not interfering.

Just documenting.

But even documentation drew reaction.

Two patrol vans tried to disperse the observers using intimidation tactics — lights, sirens, aggressive circling maneuvers.

Reign's voice came across Silk's phone:

"They testing how far they can push us."

Silk watched from a rooftop overlooking an arrest convoy.

"Don't engage," he replied. "They want reaction footage."

Reign agreed.

"Observation only. But we logging badge numbers."

Silk nodded silently.

This wasn't policing anymore.

It was suppression theater.

***

By midday…

News coverage spun fast.

HEADLINES:

CITY CRACKS DOWN ON GANG NETWORK LINKED TO PRISONER AMBUSH

Footage aired of handcuffed residents being escorted into vans — edited to look like criminal sweeps instead of community detentions.

Maya watched the broadcast in disbelief.

"They not even trying to hide the narrative twist," she said.

Dre shook his head.

"They don't have to. Fear edits perception for them."

Amina hacked into police intake logs quietly.

"They processing detainees without formal booking numbers."

Malik frowned.

"So they holding people off record?"

Dre answered:

"That means interrogation."

The room went cold.

Because everyone knew what off-record questioning meant.

***

That evening…

The retaliation reached closer to home.

A black tactical van rolled slowly past the abandoned rec center — not stopping, just scanning.

Inside, everyone froze instinctively.

Amina dimmed lights immediately.

Dre signaled silence.

The van paused for three long seconds outside.

Then continued down the block.

Malik exhaled slowly.

"They know we here."

Silk didn't look worried.

"They suspect," he corrected.

"But suspicion turns into warrants quick," Dre added.

Silk nodded.

"Which means we don't stay put long."

Maya's chest tightened.

The rec center had become more than a base.

It was safety.

Community.

Ground zero of resistance.

Leaving it meant stepping fully into the shadows.

***

Later that night…

Another call came through Silk's network.

This one darker.

"They picked up two West patrol observers," the voice said.

Silk's jaw tightened.

"Charges?"

"None filed yet."

That meant intimidation detention.

A warning shot.

He relayed the information to the crew.

"They testing unity now," he said.

"Seeing if West backs down."

Dre folded his arms.

"And if they don't?"

Silk's voice went colder.

"Then retaliation escalates again."

***

Maya sat quietly after the meeting broke.

Camera resting on her lap.

For the first time since the leak…

She wasn't filming.

She was processing.

Raids.

Detentions.

Media distortion.

Community fear.

Her footage had exposed truth…

But it had also triggered backlash.

She whispered softly:

"Did I start something I can't finish?"

Silk overheard from across the room.

He walked over slowly.

"You didn't start it," he said.

"You just turned the lights on."

She looked up at him.

"Then why it feel like people paying for my decision?"

He didn't answer immediately.

Because the truth was complicated.

Finally, he said:

"Because exposure always comes with cost."

She nodded slowly.

Then picked her camera back up.

If the city wanted to write its own narrative…

She'd film the truth louder.

Because the retaliation wave had begun.

And it wasn't slowing down anytime soon.

Chapter Eighteen

The email came at 2:11 a.m.

Encrypted.

Short.

Professional.

Subject Line:

REQUEST FOR CONFIDENTIAL INTERVIEW — PRISONER TRANSFER INCIDENT

Maya stared at the screen, heart beating faster than it should for words on a laptop.

She opened it.

"My name is Elena Navarro. I'm an investigative journalist working independent from corporate media oversight. I've reviewed fragments of leaked footage related to the Foothill transport incident. I believe the public narrative is being manipulated. If you possess additional documentation, I'd like to speak off record."

Maya read it twice.

Then a third time.

Independent.

Not corporate.

Those two words alone felt like oxygen in a suffocating room.

She forwarded the message to Amina immediately.

Within minutes, the team was awake.

***

Inside the rec center, lit only by laptop glow, the squad gathered around the folding table.

Amina pulled up Navarro's credentials.

"She's legit," Amina said. "Freelance investigative reporter. Did a series on unlawful detentions in San Diego two years ago. Won awards."

Malik leaned over her shoulder.

"So she's anti-police?"

"No," Amina corrected. "She's anti-corruption."

There was a difference.

Dre remained quiet, arms folded.

Silk watched from the back wall, unreadable.

Maya looked around the room.

"This could change everything," she said.

Dre finally spoke.

"Or expose everything."

She frowned.

"You think she's a plant?"

"I think journalists eat stories for survival," Dre said. "And we sitting on the biggest one in the city right now."

Silence followed.

Maya hated that he might be right.

But she also knew exposure required risk.

"If nobody credible reports the truth," she said, "Tate's narrative wins."

Silk nodded once.

"She meets you in public," he said. "Daytime. Controlled space. No data transfer first meeting."

Dre added:

"And we don't give her originals. Copies only."

Maya hesitated…

Then nodded.

"Alright."

The meeting was set for the next afternoon.

***

They chose Lake Merritt.

Public enough to discourage overt surveillance.

Crowded enough to disappear inside.

Elena Navarro arrived exactly on time.

Mid-30s.

Sharp eyes.

Minimal makeup.

Professional but intentionally unflashy — someone who knew blending in was protection.

She extended her hand.

"Maya?"

Maya shook it.

"Navarro?"

Elena smiled lightly.

"Call me Elena. We're on the same side here."

They walked the lake path slowly while joggers and families passed by.

No recording devices visible.

No police presence obvious.

But Maya knew better than to assume safety.

Elena got straight to it.

"I've reviewed local station footage, traffic cam stills, police statements. None of it aligns."

Maya listened carefully.

"The ballistic reports they released don't match the angles shown in public footage. And the gang narrative?" Elena shook her head. "Too clean. Too immediate."

Maya felt cautious hope rising.

"So you believe it was staged?"

"I believe," Elena said carefully, "that something happened the public hasn't been told."

She stopped walking.

Looked Maya directly in the eye.

"And I believe you have proof."

Maya hesitated.

Just long enough for instinct to whisper warnings.

But then she thought about the raids.

The detentions.

The lies already spreading unchecked.

She reached into her bag and handed Elena a flash drive.

"Partial footage," Maya said. "Not all of it."

Elena accepted it carefully.

"I'll verify authenticity before publishing anything," she said. "But if this confirms what I suspect…"

She exhaled slowly.

"This could dismantle half the department's leadership."

Maya felt something she hadn't felt in days.

Relief.

Maybe truth had found an ally.

They parted without handshake this time.

No need for optics.

Just quiet understanding.

Or so Maya thought.

***

Forty-eight hours later…

The story broke.

But not the way Maya expected.

Every major outlet ran the same headline:

LEAKED FOOTAGE SUGGESTS GANGS INFILTRATED POLICE AMBUSH

Maya stared at the television in stunned silence.

The footage airing was hers.

But edited.

Manipulated.

Frames rearranged.

Angles cropped.

Silk's face highlighted repeatedly.

Masked observers reframed as aggressors.

Police gunfire omitted entirely.

The narrative flipped completely.

"They turned it," Malik said in disbelief.

"They turned the whole damn thing."

Amina was already typing furiously.

"They didn't hack her," she said. "Metadata confirms she uploaded the edit herself."

Maya felt her stomach drop.

"No…"

Dre didn't look surprised.

"I told you," he said quietly.

But Maya barely heard him.

The broadcast cut to an interview clip.

Elena Navarro.

Professional.

Calm.

Controlled.

"What we're seeing," Elena said on screen, "is evidence that criminal organizations had advance knowledge of the transport route. While questions remain about police conduct, the primary escalation appears to have come from outside actors."

Maya's ears rang.

Outside actors.

She replayed the lake conversation in her mind.

Every word.

Every pause.

Every look.

It all felt staged now.

Weaponized trust.

"She used me," Maya whispered.

Silk muted the TV slowly.

"Not just you," he said.

"She just gave the city justification for the raids."

Amina pulled up internal police chatter intercepts.

"Retaliation warrants expanding," she read aloud. "New targets authorized based on leak confirmation."

Malik slammed his fist into the wall.

"So she fed them our footage to strengthen their case?!"

Dre nodded grimly.

"Or traded it."

The room went silent.

Because that possibility was worse.

Journalistic betrayal wasn't just narrative damage.

It was operational exposure.

***

That night…

Maya sat alone outside the rec center.

Camera beside her.

Unheld for once.

Silk approached quietly, shoulder bandaged but healing.

"You did what you thought was right," he said.

She didn't look up.

"I handed the truth to someone who sold it."

He sat beside her.

"Information war ain't about truth," he said. "It's about control."

She clenched her fists.

"She looked me in my eyes."

"And Tate probably looked Donovan in his too," Silk replied.

Trust meant nothing in this battlefield.

Maya finally looked up.

Anger replaced hurt.

"So what now?"

Silk's voice turned steel-cold.

"Now we stop asking media to tell our story."

He nodded toward her camera.

"We tell it ourselves."

She picked the camera up slowly.

Grip steady again.

Because betrayal hadn't silenced her.

It had hardened her.

And somewhere across the city…

Elena Navarro sat in a corporate studio preparing for her next segment —
unaware that she had just crossed from observer…
into participant…
in a war she didn't fully understand yet.

Chapter Nineteen

B y sunrise, Donovan was gone.

Not transferred.

Not suspended.

Not listed on administrative leave.

Gone.

His cruiser still sat in the precinct garage, parked crooked like he never finished pulling in. His locker remained half-open, uniform jacket hanging untouched, badge clipped to the pocket.

But Donovan himself?

Erased.

Dre got the confirmation through back-channel chatter before noon.

"Internal memo labeled him 'inactive pending investigation,'" Dre said, pacing the rec center floor. "That's code."

Malik looked up. "Code for what?"

Dre didn't sugarcoat it.

"Code for buried."

Silence filled the room.

Because everybody knew what that meant.

Donovan had crossed the line when he raised his weapon at Tate.

And Tate didn't leave loose ends breathing.

Maya swallowed hard.

"So either he's locked somewhere off-books…"

"Or he's already dead," Silk finished.

No one argued.

Because Silk didn't speak in hypotheticals.

He spoke in survival math.

***

But Donovan disappearing didn't calm the city.

It made things worse.

Raids increased overnight.

Unmarked vehicles.

Tactical sweeps.

Men pulled from homes without warrants.

Surveillance drones buzzing low over blocks that never saw that level of policing before.

And every operation cited the same justification:

"Gang retaliation linked to transport ambush."

Maya watched it unfold on police scanners and social feeds simultaneously — the official narrative and the street reality colliding in real time.

"They using my footage as probable cause," she said quietly.

Amina nodded grimly.

"They filed emergency public safety orders. Your video gave them legal cover."

Maya felt sick.

Her attempt at truth had been weaponized against the very people she was trying to protect.

Malik slammed his phone down.

"They hit my cousin's building last night. Tore the place apart lookin' for people that wasn't even there."

Rico added:

"They rolled through Ghost Town heavy too. Flash-bangs. Kids crying. Whole block locked down."

Silk had been silent through all of it.

Listening.

Absorbing.

Calculating.

Finally, he stood.

"They moving west now," he said.

Dre looked up sharply.

"You sure?"

Silk nodded.

"Tate expanding the map. He thinks pressure gonna flush resistance out."

Malik frowned.

"So what we do?"

Silk's eyes hardened.

"We answer."

***

West Oakland didn't mobilize loudly.

It mobilized deliberately.

Word spread through barbershops first.

Then corner stores.

Then block captains.

Then the Hyenas' extended network.

Not gangs.

Not militias.

Community protectors.

Watchers.

Drivers.

Safe house coordinators.

Silk didn't build an army.

He activated a neighborhood.

Maya rode with him that afternoon across the bridge corridor, camera in her lap, documenting everything.

Murals watched them pass.

Graffiti messages reading PROTECT THE TOWN glowed on abandoned brick.

Elders nodded at Silk as they drove by — not afraid, but

approving.

"This bigger than East," Silk told her.

"Always was."

They stopped outside an auto shop with the bay door half-open.

Inside, ten men and women stood around a folding table covered in radios, first aid kits, and street maps.

No uniforms.

No gang colors.

Just resolve.

A tall woman with silver braids stepped forward.

"You called, Silk."

He nodded respectfully.

"Raids spreading. We need watchers on rooftops, drivers on standby, med teams ready if things go left."

She didn't hesitate.

"It's already in motion."

Maya filmed quietly.

History unfolding in real time.

This wasn't chaos.

This was organized survival.

***

That night, back at the rec center, Maya sat across from Amina, footage drives spread between them.

Her jaw was set differently now.

Harder.

Resolved.

"No more waiting," Maya said.

Amina looked up.

"You sure?"

Maya nodded.

"They twisted my last leak. So this time we drop everything."

"Everything?" Malik asked from across the room.

"Uncut," Maya confirmed. "Full timeline. Police gunfire. Contractor positions. Tate's voice on comms. All of it."

Dre exhaled slowly.

"That's nuclear."

"I know," Maya said.

"But if we don't control the truth now… they bury it forever."

Silk leaned against the wall, watching her.

He saw the shift.

The poet had become a war documentarian.

"When it drops," Silk said, "it's open war narrative-wise."

Maya didn't blink.

"Then let it be open."

***

They launched it at midnight.

Not through media.

Through the streets.

Encrypted community networks.

Activist servers.

Independent livestream hubs.

Then public social platforms all at once.

Amina triggered the upload cascade.

"Mirrors active," she said. "Even if they pull one, fifty more go live."

The video spread like wildfire.

And unlike the edited leak…

This one couldn't be spun.

You saw Tate's men staging gunfire.

You saw contractors aiming at civilians.

You saw Silk dragging Briggs away without lethal force.

You saw Donovan lowering his weapon.

You saw Tate firing at Silk.

Frame by frame.

Truth unedited.

Unprotected.

Unstoppable.

***

By morning…

The city was on fire.

Protests erupted downtown.

Police headquarters barricaded itself.

City officials issued emergency press conferences calling the footage "digitally manipulated."

But too many angles existed now.

Too many witnesses.

Too many independent analysts verifying authenticity.

The narrative had split.

And once narrative fractures begin…

Control dies fast.

***

Back inside the rec center, the squad watched the coverage spiral.

Malik looked at Maya.

"You just changed the whole battlefield."

She shook her head slightly.

"No," she said.

"I just showed people where it really was."

Silk stood beside her, eyes on the screen.

"Donovan risked his life to break rank," he said quietly.

"Now the city gotta decide if it wants to hear why."

Maya tightened her grip on the camera.

Because Donovan's disappearance wasn't closure.

It was ignition fuel.

And somewhere in the shadows of West Oakland…

A rumor was already spreading:

A rogue officer was alive.

In hiding.

Preparing to testify.

Whether that rumor was hope…

or bait…

no one knew yet.

But one thing was certain:

The city had crossed the point of quiet corruption.

Now everything was public.

And public wars…

never stayed controlled for long.

Chapter Twenty

The arrest happened at 5:12 a.m.

Before sunrise.

Before the news cycle fully woke up.

Before lawyers could mobilize.

Before cameras could gather.

That was intentional.

Because when the city wanted control back, it moved in the dark.

Sirens tore through Foothill like a warning nobody had time to interpret.

Unmarked SUVs blocked both ends of the block.

Tactical units poured out — helmets, shields, rifles angled low but ready.

Neighbors' porch lights flicked on one by one.

Curtains shifted.

Phones lifted to windows.

But nobody stepped outside.

Everyone already knew:

When police show up like that, they're not there to talk.

They're there to make an example.

***

Inside the small duplex, Dre Whittaker was halfway through his morning coffee when the first door hit came.

BOOM.

The mug froze in his hand.

Second hit.

BOOM.

The frame cracked.

He didn't run.

Didn't reach for anything.

He just exhaled slowly.

"They moving fast," he muttered.

The third hit blew the door open.

Officers flooded in.

"DRE WHITTAKER! HANDS WHERE WE CAN SEE 'EM!"

He raised his hands calmly.

Didn't resist.

Didn't argue.

He knew resistance only justified violence.

They slammed him against the wall anyway.

Cuffed him anyway.

Pressed a knee into his back anyway.

Standard theater.

Standard intimidation choreography.

One officer read charges off a tablet:

"Accessory to violent gang activity. Weapons trafficking. Obstruction of police operations. Aiding prisoner escape."

Dre almost laughed.

Almost.

Because every charge was built from lies stacked on edited footage and fabricated witness statements.

"Y'all moving quick," Dre said calmly.

"We move when we need to," the officer replied.

They dragged him out of the house while neighbors recorded silently from doorways.

No shouting.

No chaos.

Just heavy, quiet witnessing.

Because the neighborhood knew:

Dre wasn't the threat.

Dre was the message.

***

By the time the news aired at 7:00 a.m., the narrative was already scripted.

"BREAKING: Key Suspect Arrested in Gang-Led Prisoner Breakout."

Maya watched the headline crawl across the TV screen in disbelief.

"They grabbed Dre?" she whispered.

Malik slammed his fist into the table.

"Of course they did. They can't find Donovan, so they grab the next closest threat."

Amina was already working.

"They filed federal holds. No bail access yet. They're trying to bury him inside the system."

Silk stood silent, jaw flexing.

He knew this move.

It wasn't about justice.

It was about optics.

Arrest someone visible.

Control the narrative.

Slow the public outrage.

But they miscalculated one thing.

They picked someone the community respected.

And that made the arrest dangerous.

For them.

***

Protests started before noon.

Small at first.

Then swelling.

Outside OPD headquarters.

Outside City Hall.

Chants rising:

"FREE DRE!"

"EXPOSE TATE!"

"WHO PROTECTS THE PEOPLE?!"

Maya filmed everything.

Not from a distance anymore.

From inside the movement.

She interviewed elders.

Youth organizers.

Former inmates who spoke about staged charges and off-books brutality.

Her camera wasn't just documenting anymore.

It was amplifying.

And every upload she dropped hit harder than the last.

***

Inside the rec center war room, tension buzzed heavy.

Malik paced nonstop.

"We can't just let him sit in there."

Rico nodded.

"They isolate him too long, they'll force a confession or make one up."

Amina added quietly:

"I'm trying to locate Donovan. If he's alive, his testimony could dismantle the charges."

Silk looked at the map spread across the table.

Then at the TV footage of protests growing outside police barricades.

Then at Maya.

"The city just escalated," he said.

"They grabbed Dre thinkin' we'd retreat."

Maya shook her head slowly.

"They grabbed Dre… and just gave us a martyr."

Silk smirked slightly.

"That's dangerous math for them."

***

By nightfall, the arrest had backfired.

Hard.

Independent journalists started dissecting Maya's leaked footage alongside Dre's charges.

Civil rights attorneys publicly questioned the legality of the arrest.

A former judge went on record calling the detainment "procedurally aggressive and politically motivated."

The more the city tried to control the story…

The faster it slipped.

***

Then came the second shock.

Amina's laptop pinged.

Encrypted channel.

Unknown sender.

She opened it carefully.

A single file loaded.

Grainy surveillance still.

Timestamped.

Underground parking structure.

And in the image…

Donovan.

Alive.

Bruised.

Being escorted by two plainclothes men into an unmarked vehicle.

Maya leaned in.

"Oh my God…"

Silk's eyes went cold.

"They didn't kill him," he said.

"They disappeared him."

Dre wasn't the real target.

Donovan was.

Because Donovan could testify.

Could expose Tate.

Could collapse the entire operation from inside.

And now…
He was off the grid.
***
Silk straightened slowly.
"This ain't about Dre no more," he said.
"It's about pulling the whole machine into daylight."
Malik looked up.
"So what's the move?"
Silk answered without hesitation.
"West mobilizes fully."
Maya tightened her grip on the camera.
"And I keep leaking."
Amina cracked her knuckles.
"And I find where they buried Donovan."
Because the city thought the first arrest would slow the resistance.
Instead…
It unified it.
Ignited it.
And accelerated the war toward something none of them could stop now.
The system had made its first public move.
And it picked the wrong man to cage.

Chapter Twenty-One

By midnight, the protests had thinned.

Not gone.

Just repositioned.

People were tired, voices hoarse, feet blistered from hours on pavement. But the energy hadn't died — it had hardened into something quieter, sharper.

Anger that didn't chant anymore.

Anger that strategized.

Inside the rec center, the war room lights stayed on.

Maps covered the folding tables.

Screens glowed.

Police band chatter crackled softly through Amina's headset.

Dre's arrest had changed the temperature of everything.

This wasn't just exposure anymore.

This was retaliation.

And retaliation required planning.

Silk stood at the center of the room, arms crossed, eyes moving across the map of downtown Oakland like he was reading pressure points on a body.

"They moved him fast," he said.

Amina nodded from behind her laptop.

"Transferred within two hours of arrest. No county holding. No intake listing."

Malik frowned.

"So where the hell he at?"

Amina rotated her screen.

"Black-site detainment facility."

Rico blinked.

"Like… CIA type?"

"Local equivalent," Amina said. "Unofficial processing locations. Used for high-sensitivity detainees before formal booking."

Maya felt her stomach drop.

"So they're isolating him."

"Interrogating him," Dre would've said if he were there.

Silk tapped the map twice.

"Where?"

Amina zoomed in.

"Old municipal records building off Mandela Parkway. Supposed to be decommissioned. Still wired. Still staffed."

Malik whistled low.

"They hid him in plain sight."

Silk nodded.

"That's Tate's style."

***

The room went quiet.

Because everyone knew what the next conversation was.

No one wanted to say it first.

Finally, Rico did.

"So… what? We breaking him out?"

Maya looked up sharply.

"That's suicide."

Silk didn't answer right away.

He studied the building schematics on the screen.

Entry points.

Security rotations.

Camera angles.

Then he spoke.

"Not a breakout," he said.

"An extraction."

Malik squinted.

"What's the difference?"

"Breakouts loud," Silk said. "Explosions. Chaos. Heat."

He tapped the screen again.

"Extractions quiet. Surgical. In and out before the system even realizes something's missing."

Amina nodded slowly.

"That building runs on a limited overnight skeleton crew. Contractors rotate perimeter. Internal security minimal after 2 a.m."

Rico cracked his knuckles.

"Minimal still means armed."

"Yeah," Silk said.

"That's why we move smart."

***

Maya stepped forward.

"Hold up," she said.

Everyone looked at her.

She swallowed but kept her voice steady.

"If we do this… we cross into their narrative."

Malik frowned.

"What you mean?"

"They already calling us terrorists," Maya said. "We storm a holding site? That validates everything they're saying."

Silk met her eyes.

"We don't storm it," he said.

"We extract one man being illegally detained."

She hesitated.

"Still looks like aggression."

"Sometimes survival looks like aggression," Silk replied quietly.

The words landed heavy.

Because they were true.

Dre didn't have weeks inside interrogation.

He barely had days.
***
Amina cleared her throat.
"There's another layer," she said.
She pulled up a secondary surveillance feed.
Grainy rooftop footage.
Two contractor teams rotating every thirty minutes.
Thermal scopes.
Military posture.
"They're guarding him like federal evidence," she said.
Silk's jaw flexed.
"That means Tate knows Dre can talk."
"And Donovan?" Maya asked.
Amina switched screens.
Another grainy still.
Same parking structure from earlier.
Same two plainclothes escorts.
Vehicle plate half-visible.
"Vehicle trace leads west," Amina said.
"Warehouse district near the port."
Silk exhaled slowly.
"They split the liabilities."
Maya pieced it together.
"Dre held central… Donovan hidden west."
"Two leverage points," Silk confirmed.
"Two extraction priorities."
***
The room fell silent again.
Because now the stakes doubled.
Malik spoke first.
"We can't hit both."
"No," Silk agreed.
"We hit Dre first. He's public. His arrest fueling protests. Pulling him out destabilizes Tate politically."
"And Donovan?" Rico asked.
Silk's eyes darkened.

"Donovan leads us to the contractors funding this whole operation."

Bigger target.

Bigger war.

***

Silk stepped forward, pointing across the building layout.

"Entry here — maintenance access."

He slid his finger.

"Exit here — underground parking ramp."

He pointed again.

"Amina cuts cameras for ninety seconds max. Any longer triggers auto-alert."

She nodded.

"I can loop footage briefly, but not forever."

Malik asked:

"And resistance?"

Silk didn't sugarcoat it.

"Contractors on outer perimeter. Internal guards armed but lighter."

Rico smirked slightly.

"So we ghost in."

Silk nodded once.

"We ghost in."

Maya's voice came quiet but firm.

"And me?"

Silk looked at her.

"You stay command-side."

She shook her head.

"No. I document."

Malik frowned.

"Maya—"

"If Dre dies in there and nobody sees how it happened," she said, "then this whole fight gets rewritten."

Silk studied her for a long moment.

Then nodded.

"You stay backline. Remote capture only. No forward movement."

She agreed.

Because she understood risk now.

She didn't need to be inside the fire to expose it.
***
They moved fast after that.

Gear checks.

Radio sync.

Vehicle assignments.

Routes plotted and memorized — not stored digitally.

By 2:10 a.m., engines idled low outside the rec center.

Silk loaded last, checking his weapon, then glancing up at Maya standing beside the passenger door.

"You scared?" he asked.

She nodded.

"Yeah."

"Good," he said softly.

"Means you understand the weight of what we about to do."

She met his eyes.

"Bring him back."

Silk gave one small nod.

"That's the only outcome I'm drivin' toward."
***
As the convoy pulled into the sleeping industrial corridor near Mandela Parkway, the city felt eerily still.

No sirens.

No foot traffic.

Just fog rolling low over asphalt and steel.

The municipal building loomed ahead — dark windows, concrete shell, quiet like it was pretending not to hold secrets.

Silk parked two blocks out.

Engines cut.

Silence took over.

He looked at the crew one last time.

"Clock starts when Amina loops the cameras."
He checked his watch.
2:37 a.m.
"This ain't revenge," he said quietly.
"This is retrieval."
Malik nodded.
Rico cracked his neck.
DeShawn checked the rear exit gear.
Amina's voice came through the comms.
"Camera loop primed… waiting on your signal."
Silk exhaled once.
Then whispered:
"Run it."
Across the block, surveillance feeds froze.
Looped.
Paused in artificial calm.
Silk looked forward.
"Move."
And just like that…
The extraction began.

Chapter Twenty-Two

The municipal records building looked dead from the outside.

No lights.

No movement.

No reason for anyone to believe human activity existed inside its concrete shell.

That was the point.

Black sites weren't meant to be visible.

They were meant to erase visibility.

Silk crouched behind a rusted utility box across the street, eyes fixed on the structure's rear maintenance entrance.

2:41 a.m.

Fog drifted low across the asphalt, thick enough to soften outlines but not thick enough to hide mistakes.

He spoke quietly into the mic.

"Perimeter check."

Rico's voice came first.

"West alley clear. One contractor rotation every thirty minutes like Amina said."

DeShawn chimed in:

"Roofline thermal sweep active. Two heat signatures posted north corner."

Malik added:

"Maintenance door in sight. No movement."

Silk nodded to himself.

"Amina, camera loop status?"

Her voice crackled softly in their ears.

"You got sixty-eight seconds before loop desync. After that I gotta reset."

Silk exhaled slowly.

"Copy."

He glanced at Malik.

"You ready?"

Malik nodded once.

"Let's go get Dre."

***

The maintenance door was secured with an electronic maglock.

Silk stepped aside as Amina's remote breach tool fed into the panel wirelessly.

Her fingers moved fast back at the rec center command station.

"Hold," she said.

Three seconds.

Five.

Seven.

Then:

"Door open. Sixty seconds."

The lock clicked.

Silk pulled the handle slowly, easing the door open just enough for the team to slip inside.

The hallway beyond was dark, lit only by emergency exit strips glowing dim red along the floor.

Old paper smell.

Dust.

But beneath it…

Fresh footsteps.

Recent activity.

Silk raised two fingers.

Move silent.

Weapons low.

They advanced single file.

***

Inside the security office, two contractors monitored blank looping camera feeds.

One frowned.

"You seeing this?" he asked.

His partner leaned closer.

"Feed looks frozen."

"Reset it."

He reached for the control panel—

And the feed snapped live again.

Except now…

Four silhouettes moved inside the building.

"Contact!" he barked, reaching for his radio.

Too late.

Rico's suppressed round shattered the office window, dropping the first contractor instantly.

The second barely turned before DeShawn breached the door, slamming him against the console hard enough to knock him unconscious.

Silent takedown.

Quick.

But not invisible anymore.

Silk checked his watch.

"We lost stealth."

Malik swallowed.

"So what now?"

Silk's eyes hardened.

"Now we move faster."

***

They descended the stairwell toward sublevel processing — Dre's most likely holding location.

The deeper they moved, the more the building felt alive.

Not active.

Aware.

Somewhere above them, alarms began to stir — not loud yet, but waking.

Silk keyed his mic.

"Amina, we tripped internal sensors."

"I see it," she said. "Lockdown initiating in ninety seconds."

"Then we got ninety seconds to grab Dre."

***

The holding corridor was colder than the rest of the building.

Concrete walls.

Steel doors.

Observation glass darkened from the inside.

Silk scanned door labels.

Temporary Processing.

Interrogation.

Isolation.

Then—

High-Security Detainment.

He stopped.

"That's him."

Rico moved to the keypad.

Amina's voice cut in:

"Stand by. I'm cracking the lock remotely."

Seconds dragged.

Malik paced.

Hearing footsteps echo somewhere down the hall.

"Anytime now," he muttered.

"Got it," Amina said.

The lock clicked.

Silk pulled the door open.

***

Dre sat cuffed to a metal chair under a single overhead light.

Bruised.

Lip split.

Eyes tired.

But alive.

He looked up slowly as they entered.

And smirked.

"Took y'all long enough."

Relief hit Malik like a wave.

"Man, we thought they buried you."

"They tried," Dre said, standing as Silk cut his restraints.

"But I ain't talk."

Silk nodded once.

"Good. Let's keep it that way. We gotta move."

As they turned to leave—

Footsteps thundered down the corridor.

Heavy.

Organized.

Contractors.

"Contact incoming!" Rico barked.

Silk shoved Dre behind cover.

"Fall back formation!"

The first contractor rounded the corner, rifle raised.

Gunfire exploded inside the narrow hall.

Muzzle flashes lit concrete walls in violent strobe bursts.

Rico returned fire, dropping one.

DeShawn pulled Dre toward the stairwell.

Malik covered rear angle.

But more boots thundered closer.

Too many.

Silk cursed under his breath.

"We got thirty seconds before full lockdown!"

Amina's voice cut in:

"Security gates sealing floors. You miss that stairwell, you trapped!"

Bullets sparked off the wall beside Silk's head.

He grabbed a smoke canister from his vest.

"Mask up!"

He tossed it down the hall.

Thick gray smoke erupted instantly, swallowing the corridor.

Visibility collapsed.

Gunfire became blind panic.

"MOVE!" Silk shouted.

They ran.

Up the stairwell.

Dre stumbling but pushing forward.

Contractors firing blindly behind them.

***

They burst out the maintenance exit just as sirens began to howl from inside the building.

Amina's voice came through:

"Camera feeds restored. You got external eyes now — move!"

They sprinted across the alley.

Vehicles already rolling forward from the pickup position.

Malik threw the rear door open.

Rico and DeShawn hauled Dre inside.

Silk jumped in last as tires screeched.

The convoy peeled away into the fog just as contractor units flooded the street behind them.

Too late.

Extraction complete.

***

Inside the moving vehicle, Dre leaned back, breathing hard.

Malik clasped his shoulder.

"You good?"

Dre nodded slowly.

"I'm good now."

He looked at Silk.

"You ain't just pull me out," he said quietly.

"You pulled the truth out with me."

Silk stared forward through the windshield.

"Truth ain't safe yet," he replied.

"Not until Donovan surfaces."

Maya's voice came over the comms from command:

"Welcome back, Dre."

Relief filled her tone.

Then hardened into resolve.
"Now we go get the rest of the truth."
Outside, the city lights blurred past the windows.
But nobody inside the vehicle felt victory yet.
Because they all knew:
Extracting Dre was only step one.
The real war was still waiting in the West.

Chapter Twenty-Three

Dre didn't sleep when they got him back to the rec center.

He tried.

Sat on the edge of the cot they'd set up in the back office, staring at the wall while Maya cleaned the dried blood from his cheek.

But every time he closed his eyes, he saw interrogation lights.

Concrete walls.

Contractor silhouettes watching through mirrored glass.

He opened his eyes again.

"I'm good," he muttered.

"You don't look good," Maya replied gently.

"I look alive," he said. "That's enough."

Across the room, Silk and Amina worked over surveillance feeds, cross-referencing contractor movements from the black site extraction fallout.

The rescue had rattled the system.

Police scanners were louder than usual.

Contractor comms spiked.

Vehicle traffic between municipal properties doubled overnight.

"They scrambling," Malik said, pacing.

"They expected Dre to stay buried longer."

Silk nodded slightly.

"They lost control of the timeline."

Amina's fingers moved across her keyboard.

"And when systems lose timeline control… they relocate assets."

She pulled up the grainy surveillance still again.

Donovan — bruised but standing — being escorted into the unmarked SUV.

She zoomed into the background.

Industrial structures.

Stacked shipping containers.

Faded port authority signage.

"I've been triangulating vehicle routes," she said.

Silk stepped closer.

"Show me."

She overlaid GPS pings from municipal contractor vehicles active the same night Donovan was taken.

Three converged.

All within the same district.

West Oakland Port Industrial Zone.

Silk exhaled slowly.

"They moved him to the docks."

Rico frowned.

"Why there?"

"Because nobody questions traffic near the port," Dre said from across the room.

All eyes turned to him.

He stood slowly, favoring his ribs but steady.

"Containers come and go all day. Contractors blend in easy. Surveillance limited. Jurisdiction messy."

Maya pieced it together.

"They didn't just hide Donovan…"

"They buried him inside logistics," Silk finished.

***

By mid-afternoon, Silk and the Hyenas' West Oakland network activated reconnaissance.

Not loud.

Not militarized.

Civilian observation.

Dock workers.

Truck dispatchers.

Night security guards.

People who had seen contractors moving where contractors didn't belong.

Maya rode shotgun again as Silk drove along West Grand Avenue toward the shipping corridors.

The skyline changed fast.

Murals gave way to cranes.

Corner stores to container stacks.

Street energy to industrial silence.

"You grew up around here?" Maya asked quietly.

Silk nodded once.

"Before the Hyenas… before everything."

He didn't elaborate.

Didn't need to.

The tension in his jaw told enough.

This wasn't just operational ground.

This was personal ground.

***

They pulled into an abandoned loading lot overlooking three warehouse rows.

A tall man in a reflective vest approached the car casually — clipboard in hand like any dock supervisor.

He leaned into the window.

"Silk."

Silk nodded back.

"Reggie."

Reggie scanned the passenger seat.

"That her? The one dropping footage?"

Maya nodded slightly.

Respect passed between them without words.

Reggie lowered his voice.

"You were right. Contractor movement heavy past three nights."
He pointed toward the far warehouse cluster.
"Building C-17. No shipping records, but trucks in and out all night."
Silk's eyes narrowed.
"Security?"
"Private perimeter. Armed. Rotating roof watch."
Maya filmed discreetly as Reggie slid Silk a folded printout.
Satellite stills.
Vehicle logs.
Entry timestamps.
"Word is," Reggie added quietly, "they holding someone important inside."
Silk nodded.
"They are."
***

Back at the rec center, the team gathered around the new intel spread across the table.
Warehouse schematics pulled from old municipal databases.
Satellite overlays.
Thermal scans Amina scraped from port security leaks.
Malik exhaled low.
"That ain't a holding site… that's a fortress."
Perimeter contractors.
Rooftop snipers.
Motion sensors at loading docks.
Armed patrol loops every ten minutes.
Rico cracked his neck.
"So extraction round two?"
Silk shook his head slightly.
"No."
All eyes turned to him.
"Dre was rescue priority," he said.
"Donovan is exposure priority."
Maya frowned.
"Meaning?"

Silk tapped the blueprint.

"If we hit this loud, Tate buries Donovan permanently."

Dre nodded slowly.

"He's more valuable alive than rescued."

Silence settled heavy.

Because that meant something harder than force.

It meant patience.

Strategy.

Evidence gathering before extraction.

***

Amina zoomed into thermal scans again.

Three heat signatures inside a reinforced subfloor unit.

Two moving.

One stationary.

"Stationary likely Donovan," she said.

Maya's chest tightened seeing the image.

He wasn't just missing.

He was imprisoned.

Alive but trapped inside the machine he tried to defect from.

Silk leaned over the table.

"We don't rush this."

Malik frowned.

"But every day he in there—"

"Is another day Tate moves assets," Silk finished.

"We need proof first. Confirmation footage. Contractor IDs. Financial ties."

Maya looked up.

"You want me to document inside."

Silk didn't hesitate.

"Yeah."

Dre exhaled.

"That's dangerous."

Maya met his gaze.

"So is silence."

The room went quiet again.

Because they all saw it now:

The poet had crossed fully into the fight.
Not as a soldier.
But as the one weapon Tate couldn't neutralize easily.
Truth.
***
As night fell, Maya stood on the rooftop across from Warehouse C-17, camera mounted low beside a ventilation unit.
She zoomed in through a high window slit.
Inside…
Contractors moved through dim corridors.
Weapons ready.
Faces hidden.
Then—
She saw him.
Donovan.
Hands bound.
Seated under interrogation lights just like Dre had been.
Her breath caught.
She kept filming.
Because this footage…
Was the key to tearing Tate's operation open from the inside.
And somewhere below…
Contractors tightened security.
Unaware that the truth had just found its lens.
The hunt wasn't about rescue yet.
It was about exposure.
And once exposure reached critical mass…
No warehouse…
No contractor unit…
No corrupt commander…
Would be able to hide from what came next.

Chapter Twenty-Four

Sergeant Nathaniel Tate didn't yell when he got the news.

He didn't slam desks.

Didn't throw anything.

Didn't rage.

He just stood in the center of the operations room, staring at the frozen surveillance still looping on the screen.

Silk.

Malik.

Rico.

DeShawn.

And Dre… being escorted out of the black site alive.

The silence around him was worse than anger.

Because everyone in the room knew:

Quiet Tate meant lethal Tate.

"How long?" he asked finally.

No one answered at first.

Lieutenant Briggs — arm in a sling from the Foothill ambush — cleared his throat.

"Seventeen minutes between camera desync and contractor response."

Tate nodded slowly.

"Seventeen minutes," he repeated.

He stepped closer to the screen.

"Enough time for amateurs to get lucky."

He zoomed the image.

Paused on Silk's face mid-exit.

Recognition flashed behind his eyes.

"Not amateurs," Tate corrected himself.

"Organized resistance."

He turned.

"Where's Donovan?"

The room stiffened.

One contractor liaison spoke carefully.

"Still secured at port detainment location."

"Still?" Tate asked.

The man swallowed.

"We had surveillance breach attempts on Warehouse C-17 rooftop last night."

That made Tate's eyes narrow.

"Visual confirmation?"

"Unclear. Possible independent journalist activity."

Tate smirked faintly.

"Journalist…"

He knew better.

This wasn't media curiosity.

This was coordinated intelligence gathering.

Dre free.

Donovan observed.

Footage leaking.

The resistance wasn't reacting anymore.

They were building a case.

And that made them more dangerous than any gang unit he'd ever dismantled.

Because gangs fought territory.

This group fought truth.

***

Tate stepped away from the screens.

"Contractor command online?" he asked.

A voice answered through the encrypted comm console.

"Here."

Tate spoke evenly.

"Upgrade operational status."

Silence for half a beat.

Then:

"Confirm escalation parameters."

Tate didn't hesitate.

"Authorize full-spectrum counterinsurgency."

Briggs looked up sharply.

"That's heavy, Nate."

Tate didn't look at him.

"They extracted a detainee from a secured black site," Tate said calmly.

"They infiltrated contractor surveillance grids. They're documenting operations."

He finally turned.

"This isn't civil unrest anymore. This is organized insurgency."

No one argued.

Because from his perspective…

He wasn't wrong.

"Greenlight surveillance sweeps across East and West sectors," Tate continued.

"Drones, facial recognition pulls, license plate nets."

The contractor liaison added:

"And resistance leaders?"

Tate's answer came cold.

"Neutralize if necessary."

The room fell silent.

Because neutralize didn't mean arrest.

It meant eliminate.

***

By nightfall, the counterstrike began.

Unmarked drones buzzed over rec center corridors.

License plate scanners tracked Hyena vehicles across city blocks.

Plainclothes units trailed community organizers leaving protest sites.

And contractors repositioned around Warehouse C-17 with doubled security layers.

Inside the warehouse, Donovan sat chained beneath interrogation lights as Tate's new orders reached the facility.

A contractor stepped inside.

"Command wants accelerated extraction of testimony."

Donovan looked up through swollen eyes.

"You mean torture," he rasped.

The contractor didn't deny it.

"Compliance is advised."

Donovan leaned back slowly.

"Tell Tate something for me."

The contractor paused.

"What?"

Donovan smirked faintly despite the pain.

"You can bury me… but you can't bury what I already told."

The contractor's expression shifted slightly.

Because that sentence carried weight.

If Donovan had already spoken…

Then Tate's operation was already compromised.

***

Across town, the squad felt the pressure almost immediately.

Amina tracked the surveillance spikes first.

"We're being mapped," she said.

"How mapped?" Malik asked.

"Full grid. Devices, vehicles, movement patterns."

Dre exhaled.

"He escalated."

Silk stood by the window, watching drones pass overhead like mechanical vultures.

"He's not hunting randomly," Silk said quietly.

"He's hunting leadership."

Maya looked up from her editing station.

"You."

Silk didn't respond.

But he didn't deny it either.

***

Then came the first direct strike.

A West Oakland safe house Silk's network used for med staging got hit just after midnight.

Contractors stormed the location.

Flash-bangs.

Tactical entry.

No arrests.

Just destruction.

Equipment smashed.

Surveillance wiped.

Message sent.

By the time Silk's drivers reached the scene, contractors were already gone.

No bodies.

No survivors needed.

Just intimidation.

Silk stood in the wreckage, jaw tight.

"He's not trying to stop us," Malik said.

"He's trying to scare the city back into silence."

Silk shook his head slowly.

"No," he said.

"He's trying to provoke us into moving sloppy."

He looked at the shattered equipment.

"At making mistakes."

***

Back at the rec center, Maya finished compiling the rooftop surveillance footage she'd captured of Donovan.

She layered it beside Dre's extraction testimony.

Contractor IDs.

Vehicle plates.

Interrogation timestamps.

The case file was building faster than Tate could bury it.

But now the risk multiplied.

Because Tate knew they had evidence.

And that made Maya just as dangerous as any armed operative.

She looked up at Silk.

"If he's counterstriking… he's coming for the footage next."

Silk nodded.

"Which means he's coming for you."

The weight of that landed differently than it would've weeks ago.

Maya didn't flinch now.

Didn't retreat.

She just saved the files to five separate encrypted drives.

Then looked back at him.

"Then we leak before he can silence it."

Silk watched her a moment.

Saw the evolution complete.

The poet had become the archive.

The witness.

The one thing Tate couldn't assassinate without proving everything she exposed.

***

Across the bay, Tate stood alone in the operations room again, watching new drone feeds populate across the city grid.

Resistance movement patterns.

Hyena transport routes.

Rec center surveillance snapshots.

He zoomed in on Maya's face captured entering the building hours earlier.

"Documentarian," he murmured.

Then Silk.

"Strategist."

Then Malik.

"Connector."

He leaned back slightly.

"Cut the head," he whispered to himself.

"The body collapses."

Outside, sirens rose again across Oakland's night skyline.

The counterstrike had begun.

And it wouldn't stop until either the resistance broke…

Or Tate's entire machine collapsed under the weight of the truth coming for it.

Chapter Twenty-Five

The moment Maya hit **RUN**, the room didn't celebrate. It went silent. Because everyone understood something at a primal level:

They hadn't ended anything. They had just fired the first global shot.

At first, nothing happened. Just server lights blinking. Upload bars crawling. Encrypted mirrors bouncing signals offshore.

Then—

Amina's screen flickered.

"Primary mirror live."

Another screen.

"Secondary leak channel active."

Then another.

"International relay engaged."

The progress bar hit 22%.

Then 37%.

Then 61%.

Maya's heart pounded so loud she could hear it in her ears.

"Contractor firewall trying to block," Amina muttered, typing fast. "They're throttling bandwidth."

Dre leaned in.

"Can they stop it?"

Amina didn't look up.

"They can slow it…"

Her fingers flew faster.

"…but they can't stop what's already multiplying."

The bar hit 83%.

Across every screen in the rec center—

Feeds began lighting up. News tickers. Independent journalists. Encrypted activist streams. Legal watchdog portals. The footage was no longer uploading. It was spreading. Uncontrollably.

———

Detonation.

———

Within minutes:

Oakland local stations broke first.

"—leaked footage appears to show unauthorized contractor detainment—"

Then regional networks:

"—black-site interrogation tied to private security coalition—"

Then national:

"—federal oversight agencies reviewing classified operations—"

And then—

International.

Human rights coalitions began mirroring the footage faster than takedown requests could move.

Amina stared at the cascade.

"It's wildfire now."

———

Cut to Warehouse C-17.

Contractor command screens began lighting up red.

"Sir — we've got media breaches."

"How many?"

"Too many."

Screens flashed interrogation clips.
Drone footage overlays.
Financial trails.
Donovan's battered face staring into camera.
The commander swore under his breath.
"Shut it down."
"We're trying — mirrors are offshore."
"Then jam signal!"
"We can't jam the internet!"
Panic crept in.
Because this wasn't a battlefield anymore.
It was exposure.

———

Outside the warehouse—
Sniper teams began receiving new radio chatter.
"Command revising engagement protocol."
"Define revise."
"…Stand by."
Gun barrels that had been aimed at kill zones now hesitated mid-scope.

———

Inside the holding bay, Donovan heard the shift instantly.
Aggression left the air like a vacuum seal breaking.
No boots rushing him.
No fists.
No interrogation lights snapping on.
Just tense whispers.
Legal language.
Risk calculations.
He smirked through split lips.
"They see you now," he rasped.

———

Back at the rec center—
Cheers almost broke out when federal alerts hit the news crawl.
But Dre didn't smile.
He stepped toward the surveillance wall.

"Zoom port grid."
Rico complied.
Drone feeds expanded across the monitors.
Contractor convoys were moving.
Not retreating.
Repositioning.

———

"Why they shifting west?" Malik asked.
Amina's fingers froze over the keyboard.
Her voice dropped.
"…Because municipal jurisdiction ends there."
Silk's jaw tightened.
"Private port authority zones."
Dre nodded slowly.
"No warrants. No oversight. No press access."
Maya looked up.
"They're relocating the operation."
Silk finished the thought cold:
"Exposure didn't stop the machine…"
He watched armored trucks disappear into deeper dock sectors.
"…it forced it underground."

———

Suddenly—
Police scanners erupted across Rico's console.
"Downtown protest surge escalating!"
Feed switched live.
Thousands filled the streets now.
Chants thundered off buildings:
"EXPOSE THEM ALL!"
"JUSTICE FOR THE EAST!"
Police barricades strained under the swell.
Flashbangs popped in the distance.
Helicopters cut lower.
Oakland wasn't watching anymore.
Oakland was moving.

———

Silk grabbed his comm.

"All Hyena units — shift protest perimeter support. Keep civilians shielded. No escalation unless fired upon."

Acknowledgments crackled back.

The resistance wasn't hiding anymore either.

They were standing in daylight.

———

Inside C-17—

Contractor teams began dismantling interrogation rigs.

Not out of mercy.

Out of liability.

"Legal wants all enhanced methods halted immediately."

One guard unlocked Donovan's shackles from the floor ring — but left his wrists bound.

Procedure shift.

Not freedom.

Donovan flexed numb fingers.

"Running already?" he muttered.

The guard avoided eye contact.

That told him everything.

———

Back downtown—

Tear gas rolled through protest lines.

But instead of scattering—

Crowds locked arms.

Phones raised.

Livestreams active.

The entire confrontation broadcast in real time.

Police tactics restrained themselves mid-motion.

Because now the watchers were watching the watchers.

———

At the rec center—

Maya filmed the live feeds compiling evidence in real time.

Her voice barely above a whisper:

"This isn't documentation anymore…"

Dre glanced at her.

"What is it?"
She didn't look away from the screen.
"…it's battlefield recording."

———

Silk stood at the window overlooking the city skyline.
Helicopters still circling.
Sirens still screaming.
But something had shifted in the air.
Tate had lost invisibility.
But not power.

———

Dre joined him.
"So what now?"
Silk didn't answer immediately.
His eyes tracked a contractor convoy vanishing into the western dock shadows.
Finally:
"Now he does something desperate."

———

Cut to an undisclosed command center.
Dark.
Minimal lighting.
Multiple screens replaying the leaked footage.
A figure stood in silhouette watching Donovan's interrogation loop.
Unmoving.
Unshaken.
Tate.
A subordinate spoke carefully behind him.
"Sir… federal inquiries are initiating."
Tate didn't turn.
"And the warehouse?"
"Standing down from lethal authorization."
Silence.
Then Tate spoke — calm, controlled, colder than before:
"Good."

The subordinate blinked.

"Sir?"

Tate finally turned slightly.

"If they think exposure ends this…"

His eyes hardened.

"…they misunderstand escalation."

He faced the screens again.

"Prepare Phase Two."

————

Back in Oakland—

Night fell.

But the city didn't sleep.

Protests burned brighter under streetlights.

Helicopters hovered like mechanical vultures.

Contractor units fortified deeper port sectors beyond oversight reach.

And inside Warehouse C-17—

Donovan sat upright now.

Listening.

Waiting.

Because he could feel it too.

The storm hadn't passed.

It had widened.

————

Final closing beat:

Oakland didn't wake up that morning.

It braced.

By nightfall—

It was standing in the middle of a war no one could hide anymore.

And somewhere in the shadows beyond the port lights…

The next strike was already in motion.

Chapter Twenty-Six

No celebrations happened at the rec center that night.
No victory speeches.
No relief.

Because everyone who had lived long enough in Oakland knew one truth:

Exposure doesn't end power.

It provokes it.

———

Three hours after the global leak—
Amina's intrusion alarms went off.
Not loud.
Subtle.
Which made it worse.
She froze over her keyboard.
"…They're inside."
Dre turned instantly.
"Inside what?"
"Our mirrors. Not shutting them down… mapping them."
Silk stepped closer.
"Tracing us?"

Amina nodded slowly.
"They're learning how we move."

———

Across the port district—
Contractor convoys that had relocated west weren't sitting idle.
They were restructuring.
New barricades.
New signal jammers.
Unregistered drones lifting into the air under private jurisdiction clearance.
No media allowed.
No warrants required.
A war zone without witnesses.

———

Inside Warehouse C-17—
Donovan's holding room door opened.
But it wasn't interrogation staff.
It was transport.
Black tactical gear.
No insignias.
One guard cut his restraints loose from the chair.
"On your feet."
Donovan frowned.
"Where we going?"
The guard didn't answer.
That silence said enough.
They weren't holding him anymore.
They were moving him somewhere no cameras could reach.

———

Back at the rec center—
Rico's drone feed suddenly fuzzed out over the western port grid.
"Signal jammed."
Amina's face tightened.
"They're blacking out that entire sector."
Silk looked at the dead screen.

"That ain't defensive…"
Dre finished the thought:
"That's preparation."

———

Then Maya's phone buzzed.
Unknown encrypted drop.
She opened it cautiously.
A single video file.
No sender ID.
No traceable metadata.
She hit play.

———

The footage showed a dimly lit room.
Concrete walls.
Industrial lighting.
A chair bolted to the floor.
And sitting in it—
One of their own.
Bruised.
Restrained.
Alive.
But captured.
The camera slowly zoomed closer.
Then a voice spoke from off-screen.
Calm.
Controlled.
Ice cold.
Tate.
"You wanted the world watching…"
A pause.
"…now watch closely."
The feed cut to static.

———

Back in the rec center—
No one moved.
No one spoke.

Because the message wasn't ransom.
It wasn't negotiation.
It was demonstration.
Tate hadn't lashed out blindly.
He'd selected a piece from their board.
And removed it.

———

Silk exhaled slow.
"Phase Two."
Dre's jaw tightened.
"He's hunting now."
Amina whispered:
"And he knows where to look."

———

Cut to Tate's undisclosed command center.
He watched protest footage on one screen.
Federal investigations on another.
But his focus stayed on the third—
The rec center surveillance still frame he'd captured earlier that night.
Mapped.
Tagged.
Studied.
A subordinate stepped beside him.
"Sir… public pressure is mounting."
Tate didn't look away.
"Good."
The subordinate hesitated.
"Good… sir?"
Tate's voice lowered.
"Pressure makes resistance predictable."
He turned slightly.
"And predictable enemies are easier to dismantle."

———

Back in Oakland—
Protests still roared downtown.

Helicopters still circled.
News stations still ran the leak on repeat.
To the public—
It looked like the resistance had gained ground.
But inside the rec center—
They knew the truth.
They hadn't weakened the machine.
They'd triggered its war protocol.

———

Final closing paragraph energy:
Oakland didn't wake up that morning.
It braced.
By nightfall, the world was watching the city fight in the open.
But somewhere beyond the protest lights…
Beyond the cameras…
Beyond federal jurisdiction…
Tate was already making his next move.
And this time—
He wasn't defending power.
He was preparing to erase anyone who threatened it.
The war for The East had just entered a phase no exposure could stop.
And the next strike…
Was already in motion.

Epilogue

The footage didn't just shake Oakland.

It rippled outward. National outlets ran the story for days — looping contractor gunfire, Dre's testimony, Donovan's interrogation clips, Tate's unit coordinating off-books operations.

Civil rights coalitions demanded federal intervention.

Oversight committees launched preliminary inquiries.

City Hall scrambled to distance itself from tactical decisions it had quietly funded months earlier.

Publicly, the machine cracked.

Privately…

It adapted.

Because systems like Tate's weren't built to collapse.

They were built to mutate.

***

Sergeant Nathaniel Tate disappeared three days after the leak.Officially, he was placed on administrative suspension pending federal review.

Unofficially…

His residence was cleared overnight.

Bank accounts emptied.

Digital footprint scrubbed clean. By the time investigators arrived with warrants, the house felt staged — furniture still in place, lights left on, but nothing personal left behind.

He hadn't fled in panic.

He had withdrawn strategically.

Like a commander relocating to a secondary theater.

Silk watched the news report from the rec center war room, arms crossed.

"He didn't run," Silk said quietly.

"He repositioned."

Dre nodded.

"Tate answers to someone. Men like him don't disappear without protection waiting."

Maya filmed the coverage, archiving every public reaction, every denial statement, every political pivot.

Because she understood now:

Exposure was only phase one.

Accountability was phase two.

And phase two always met resistance.

***

Donovan remained officially "missing."

No department statement confirmed his detainment.

No facility admitted custody.

But Maya's rooftop footage kept circulating online — showing his silhouette inside Warehouse C-17 beneath interrogation lights.

Public pressure mounted daily.

Civil attorneys filed emergency writs demanding proof-of-life hearings.

Contractor firms named in the footage issued statements denying involvement — while quietly relocating assets out of Oakland jurisdiction.

And still…

Donovan wasn't released.

Which meant he was still leverage.

Still a liability.

Still alive.

But buried deeper.

***

West Oakland moved differently after the leak.

Quieter.

More organized.

More watchful.

Silk's network expanded beyond neighborhood defense.

Dock unions coordinated movement tracking.

Truck drivers flagged contractor shipments.

Port security insiders leaked shift rotations.

Community protection turned into intelligence infrastructure. Maya rode through the district again weeks later, filming recovery murals being painted across warehouse walls. Images of Dre. Of protestors. Of cameras raised instead of weapons. Of the words:

THE TRUTH SURVIVED.

She lowered the camera as Silk parked near the waterline overlooking the shipping cranes.

"You feel it?" he asked.

"Feel what?"

"The shift."

She nodded slowly.

"Yeah."

Because East Oakland had resisted.

But West Oakland…

Was preparing.

***

That night, Silk entered a building he hadn't stepped foot in for years. An old maritime union hall — long abandoned publicly, but still active behind closed doors.

Inside, twelve figures sat around a long wooden table.

No gang colors.

No badges.

No introductions.

Just power.

A gray-haired man at the head spoke first.

"You stirred federal attention," he said.

Silk didn't sit.

"Did what needed to be done."

Another voice cut in:

"Tate was just enforcement. Contractors just muscle."

Silk's eyes narrowed.

"Then who funding the purge?"

The gray-haired man slid a thin dossier across the table.

Inside:

Private security conglomerate shell companies.

Real estate acquisition maps.

Port redevelopment zoning approvals.

Political donors tied to surveillance contracts.

The purge wasn't about revenge for dead officers.

It was about clearing land.

Clearing resistance.

Clearing communities for redevelopment corridors stretching from East Oakland into the port.

Silk closed the file slowly.

"So Tate wasn't the architect," he said.

"He was the weapon."

The man nodded.

"And the hand holding that weapon…"

He tapped the map.

"…is headquartered right here in the West."

***

Back at the rec center, Maya reviewed the new footage she'd been compiling — protest victories, federal inquiries, community rebuilding.

But something in her expression had changed.

She wasn't documenting aftermath anymore.

She was documenting prelude.

Dre stepped beside her.

"You thinking about what comes next."

She nodded.

"This wasn't the war," she said.

"This was the warning."

He looked at the skyline through the window — cranes blinking red over the port horizon.

"And warnings only matter," he said, "if people listen."

Maya lifted the camera again.

Zooming toward the industrial district where contractor lights still glowed behind reinforced fencing.

"I'm still listening," she said quietly.

***

Miles away, in a private terminal office overlooking container ships moving through the bay, a man watched the same protest footage Maya had been filming.

He wasn't military.

Wasn't police.

Didn't wear tactical gear.

He wore a tailored suit.

Calm.

Detached.

Interested.

A contractor liaison entered the room.

"Sir… Tate has gone dark."

The man nodded.

"He served his function."

"And the resistance network?"

The man watched Maya's footage on the screen — her camera steady in the face of police lines.

He smiled faintly.

"Every conflict needs a face," he said.

"And now we know theirs."

He turned back toward the window overlooking West Oakland's port grid.

"Begin Phase Two," he said quietly.

Below him, cargo cranes moved silently in the night.

Containers shifting.

Territory reshaping.

War evolving.

***

Back in East Oakland, Maya finished filming one last skyline shot before lowering her camera.

Sirens still echoed.

Drones still hummed.

Contractor lights still burned in the distance.

But the city felt awake now.

Not afraid.

Aware.

She whispered into the recorder:

"This is not the end of the story."

She looked west toward the port.

"It's the beginning of the next one."

And somewhere across that dark industrial horizon…

The West was already moving.

Acknowledgments

First and foremost, I want to give honor to God for the vision, the breath, and the endurance to see this story through. This book was built on faith, reflection, and purpose — and without that foundation, none of these pages would exist.

To my family — thank you for your patience, your love, and your understanding during the long nights of writing, rewriting, and disappearing into this world. Your support kept me grounded while I poured pieces of myself into every chapter.

To the City of Oakland — especially the East. Every block, every street corner, every lesson — good and bad — shaped this story. This book is a reflection of the soil that raised me. The culture, the codes, the survival, the loyalty… it all lives here. Seminary, Bancroft, Foothill, 60th, 73rd — this is our narrative, told with truth and respect.

To the homies, the day-ones, and those no longer with us — your stories, your energy, and your memories echo through these pages. Some of you inspired characters directly, others inspired the spirit of the book. Either way, your imprint is permanent.

To the readers — thank you for taking this ride with me. Whether you're from Oakland or just stepping into this world for the first time, I appreciate you investing your time and imagination into this story.

To everyone building, creating, and striving to turn pain into purpose — this series is for you.

And finally, to the storytellers who came before me — the ones who showed that our voices, our streets, and our truth deserve to live in print — thank you for opening the door.

Welcome to **The East.**

— **Chrome Nyson**

Also by Chrome Nyson

The Oakland Trilogy

Oakland – Book One: The East

Oakland – Book Two: The West *(Coming Soon)*

Oakland – Book Three: The North *(Coming Soon)*

———

Stand-Alone & Connected Works

Oakland – Book Four: Seminary Ave

———

Upcoming Projects

Additional titles from the Oakland story universe are currently in development, continuing the legacy, streets, and survival codes that define **The Town**.

Stay connected for release updates, soundtrack drops, and film adaptations tied to the Oakland series.

———

Chrome Nyson

An Orline Media Literary Brand